D.R. GRAHAM

D.R. Graham lives in Vancouver, Canada with her husband. She worked as a social worker with at-risk youth prior to becoming a therapist in private practice. Her novels deal with issues relevant to young adults in love, transition, or crisis.

www.drgrahambooks.com

Other books by D.R. Graham:

And Then What?

Britannia Beach

D.R. GRAHAM

A division of HarperCollins*Publishers*
www.harpercollins.co.uk

HarperImpulse an imprint of
HarperCollinsPublishers
1 London Bridge Street
London SE1 9GF

www.harpercollins.co.uk

A Paperback Original 2016

First published in Great Britain in ebook format by HarperImpulse 2016

A catalogue record for this book
is available from the British Library

ISBN: 9780008145217

This novel is entirely a work of fiction.
The names, characters and incidents portrayed in it are
the work of the author's imagination. Any resemblance to
actual persons, living or dead, events or localities is
entirely coincidental.

Set in Minion by Palimpsest Book Production Ltd, Falkirk, Stirlingshire

Printed and bound in Great Britain

Fi...

For anyone going through a rough time

Chapter 1

Every glass and mirrored surface in my mom's high-rise condo was sparkling by the time I finished rushing around with a spray bottle. My boyfriend's best friend, Murphy, was seated on the leather couch flicking between a football and a hockey game on TV. The party was about to start and I hadn't even changed yet, so I handed him the broom. "Murph, a little help? Please and thank you."

Despite the fact that his focus didn't leave the television, he heaved his giant frame off the couch and half-heartedly pushed the broom over the hardwood floors as I quickly fluffed the throw pillows and stashed one of my textbooks under the couch. The original plan was to celebrate Trevor's twenty-first birthday party up in Britannia Beach on the actual date, but then I got the bright idea to push it two weeks earlier and host it in Vancouver so he would be surprised. Too bad I didn't factor into account that I'd have two papers due, a group project, and an exam while I was trying to plan everything. Sleep is overrated anyway, right?

"The place is already spotless, Deri." Murphy said. "It's not like Trevor cares what it looks like."

"The thirty other people who are about to show up will." The doorbell rang right on cue.

Trevor's sister Kailyn, who was blowing up balloons at the dining table, sprung up and answered the door for me. It was her dad, so she gave him a hug around his waist.

"Hi everyone." Jim Maverty waved, removed his jacket and shoes, then crossed the room and sat down on the couch to watch the game Murphy had left on. He wasn't an overly chatty guy and social gatherings weren't really his thing. He only came down to Vancouver from Britannia Beach for special occasions.

"Mom!" I hollered down the hall towards her bedroom as I turned the stereo system on for background music. "Jim's here."

"Okay, I'll be right out."

My best friend, Sophie, was helping my granddad prepare the hors d'oeuvres in the kitchen. She had moved back home from New York at the end of December after the off-Broadway play she'd been singing in ended its run. Her boyfriend, Doug asked her to move in with him in Los Angeles, but she hadn't yet because he was on a world tour with his band and wouldn't be back for another three months. In the meantime she was living at her parents' house in Squamish and working as a waitress in Whistler, which she wasn't crazy about. I tugged the loose braid she'd woven her long black hair into. "Mmm, that bruschetta smells amazing." I popped a spinach, tomato, and feta-covered piece of bread into my mouth. "It tastes amazing too. Thanks for helping with the food. You're a life-saver."

"I've been doing more eating than helping. Your grandpa did most of the work." She dumped half a bottle of barbecue sauce over a dish of chicken wings.

It had been over a month since I'd seen Granddad because I had been swamped with school work. Originally, when I had decided to stay in Vancouver and attend the same school as Trevor, I had hoped to go up to Britannia Beach on weekends to visit Granddad, Sophie, and Kailyn, but finding the time turned out to be harder than I thought it would be. Going from seeing him every day for my entire life to less than once a month made me sad. I hugged him and kissed his cheek. "Thanks, Granddad. I've missed you."

"I've missed you, too." He opened the oven door and slid in a baking sheet of about fifty mini quiches. "But stop hovering. You can go get ready. We have everything under control in here."

"Okay, thanks." I had been hovering and micro-managing too much. I wanted everything to be perfect, but I hadn't scheduled enough time for perfection. All Trevor would care about was having his friends and family around to celebrate. It was me who wanted it to feel like a proper, sophisticated grown-up party. I leaned my palms on the granite countertop of the kitchen island, poked my head out towards the living room. "Can I get anyone a drink or a meatball or something?"

The doorbell rang again and Kailyn got up to answer it.

"We're fine, Deri. Just go get ready," Murphy said.

I did need to get changed, so I left everything in their capable hands. On the way to my room, my mom passed me in the hall, putting her earring in and pressing her lips together to blend her lipstick. She looked nice.

"Is Ron coming?" I asked her.

"No, sweetheart. I know you don't feel comfortable when he's here."

True. He'd been her boyfriend for almost a year, but it still didn't sit right with me. Feeling guilty for being childish about their relationship, I tucked my hair behind my ears and attempted to come across as more mature than I actually was. "You could have invited him to the party. I just feel weird when he's hanging around here without you as if he lives here."

"Maybe with more time you'll get used to him."

"Yeah, time," I said under my breath. Although I really had no choice but to accept that she and Ron were a thing, I couldn't imagine ever being comfortable with him lounging around on the couch and helping himself to food and trying to have parental-type talks with me. I wasn't ready for that. Hard to host a grown-up party if I couldn't even be adult enough to accept the fact that my mom had a boyfriend, though. "Call him and tell him he's welcome."

"I think he made plans with his son, but I'll let him know." Mom touched my arm lightly, then carried on down the hall to join everyone in the living room. Ron's son was seventeen and already cool with my mom, which she reminded me of frequently. His situation was different, though. His parents divorced when he was five years old. My parents adored each other and would have still been together if my dad hadn't died in a car crash when I was fifteen. Change really wasn't my thing. Admittedly, I needed to work on letting things go.

Later.

Voices filled the living room as more people arrived, so I ducked into my room. The black, fitted dress I'd borrowed from Sophie was hung on the back of my closet door. I really wanted the party to be a success because, despite going to the same school, Trevor and I had barely seen each other in weeks. I missed him. I brushed my hair, applied a little makeup, stepped into the dress, and slipped my feet into black pumps—all in record time. Ugh, I shouldn't have looked in the mirror. Three nights in one week of pulling all-nighters to finish my assignments were not kind to me.

The doorbell rang again as I crossed my room to get Trevor's birthday gift out of the drawer of my bedside table. It had slid next to the box where I kept the necklace Mason gave me. Mason and I had dated right after I graduated from high school, and although it hadn't lasted long and I hadn't seen him since, I never forgot about him. I stared for a second at the two boxes sitting next to each other, then picked up the box that had Trevor's gift in it. He was supposed to arrive in five minutes, so I hurried back out into the living room.

Murphy whistled when he saw me. "You clean up good."

I rolled my eyes in a self-deprecating gesture as my cheeks

heated. "Thanks. Can I get anyone a drink?" I asked to avoid being the centre of attention. Nobody took me up on my offer, so I stacked the gift on the kitchen island with the others and fidgeted with my dress to make it hang right. The condo was maybe not designed to be crammed with so many bodies. It was sweltering. It might have been just me. I waved my hands in front of my face to cool myself off.

Sophie sat on a stool next to the island. "Derian, relax. Everything's ready, the place looks great, and you look hot."

"Right, relax. I'm getting too worked up, aren't I?"

"Yes," Sophie and my mom both said in unison.

"This probably wasn't the best week to plan a surprise party," I admitted. "Exam worth fifty percent of my mark, three assignments, and I haven't even thought about packing for our trip to Tofino yet. I may have been a little too ambitious when I decided to invite everyone we know over on such short notice."

"The hard part's done. All you need to do now is enjoy yourself," my mom reassured me.

"You're right. This will be good. Last term was busy for both Trevor and me, but my assignments are all handed in, my exam is over—although I'm not sure I did that well—and I can pack for Tofino tomorrow. It will be nice to just have fun. Okay, I'm calming down. I can do this."

Sophie looked at me as if she knew there was something more wrong with me than just the stress of the party, but she didn't ask. Truthfully, she was right. My high-strung mood had more to do with a vision I'd had earlier, but exhaustion, unrealistic expectations, and an over-estimation of what I was capable of achieving weren't helping either.

"How's Doug?" I asked to turn the focus away from me.

Sophie shrugged and transferred some turkey meatballs into a serving dish. She stabbed a toothpick into each one with more force than was necessary. "Good, I guess. The band is playing in Moscow tonight."

"Cool. Where's the next stop on the tour?"

"Berlin."

"Did he get all his stuff moved into his new condo before they had to leave?"

"No. His assistant is finishing everything while he's gone." She stabbed the last couple of toothpicks with increasing force.

"Assistant? Wow. When did he get an assistant?"

She shrugged and poured herself a glass of wine. I was going to ask more questions, but she walked away and took the bottle with her into the living room to top up other people's glasses. Murphy's girlfriend Rene had arrived. Although she normally drank wine, she politely declined and then smiled adoringly at Murphy. He stretched his massive arm across her shoulder to squeeze her into his side, looking all proud. Whoa. I made eye contact with him in an attempt to ask with my expression if that gesture meant what I thought it meant, and if it did mean that, did Trevor know? He shot me an amused but otherwise unrevealing look. The timer buzzed for the quiches. He was saved by the bell. Temporarily. I planned to get to the bottom of that exchange. I rushed into the kitchen and took the quiche out of the oven, then slid the tins of apple-cinnamon muffins in—an unconventional replacement for a birthday cake, but they were my specialty and Trevor's favourite. The recipe was originally my grandmother's, and ever since he moved to Britannia Beach when he was seven years old, Trevor would come over to the Inn each morning for a fresh, home-made, apple-cinnamon muffin.

The condo was packed and getting hotter. I opened the sliding glass door that led to the patio and took a few deep breaths of the cool, rainy spring air. Murphy walked past me into the kitchen to load up a plate with chicken wings.

I spun around and rested my butt on the counter, with my arms crossed. In some ways it was bizarre to think of someone the same age as Trevor already being a dad. But I'd known

Murphy since he and Trevor became best friends as kids, and Murphy had always been both big and mature for his age. He'd moved out of his mom's house when he was seventeen. Then, after he graduated high school, he went straight into training at the Justice Institute and already had a stable career as a paramedic. Rene was twenty-four and a nurse, who owned her own place. It made sense that they were in a position to start a family. If that's what their knowing look was about. "So, anything new with you and Rene?"

"Nope. Same old same old." He tossed a cherry tomato up in the air and caught it in his mouth.

"Are you sure? Nothing new? Nothing developing?"

He smiled and shook his head to deny it. His smile is what gave him away.

"Oh my God, Murphy. That is so exciting."

He held his hands up in defense. "What's so exciting? I don't know what you're talking about. I didn't say anything."

I lunged over and hugged him around the waist. "Have you told Trevor yet?"

"Uh." He glanced over his shoulder. "There's nothing to tell. Are you having one of your Spidey senses or something?"

"No. I had a vision this morning but it wasn't about you and Rene. I just noticed that she's not drinking and you look all happy and goofy. There's something to tell, isn't there?"

He rolled his eyes and twisted the cap off a beer. "Zip it."

I bounced up and down on my toes, about to burst from the news. "When can I unzip it?"

He shook his head in an attempt to discourage my enthusiasm as Rene joined us in the kitchen. He shot me a cautionary glare.

She smiled and slid in next to him. "Sorry to interrupt, but I have to go to back to work soon. What time is Trevor supposed to arrive?"

"Eight." I looked at the clock on the stove, which showed eight forty-five. "What time do you have?" I asked Murphy.

He took his phone out of his pocket and glanced at the screen. "Eight forty-five."

"Are you sure?"

We both knew it was out of character for Trevor to be late, but Murphy said, "He probably got caught up in traffic."

"For forty-five minutes? He would have called if he was going to be this late." I texted him to ask if he was on his way.

Murphy's eyes darted away from mine. He knew I was right.

"He'll be here." Murphy reached across the counter, grabbed a couple of pieces of sushi, and popped them both into his mouth, probably so he wouldn't be able to say anything. He glanced at me one more time, then stretched his arm across Rene's shoulder and walked away.

Trevor still hadn't responded to my text when Sophie stepped into the kitchen to get a new bottle of wine. She had on a black mini skirt and she'd put on one of my mom's frilly white aprons so she looked like a French maid. The guys seemed to be enjoying it.

"Rene's not drinking," she said with a curious eyebrow lift.

Partly to avoid divulging anything Murphy wouldn't want me to, and partly because I was actually starting to worry, I said, "Trevor's almost an hour late."

She waved her hand to dismiss my concern. "Don't worry about it. You know what he's like. He probably came across an accident and helped some people who needed saving or something. What did you tell him you guys were going to be doing?"

"Nothing specific. I didn't want to sound suspicious, so I just said come over around eight."

"Maybe he didn't realize it was a set plan. Just call him."

"Okay, yeah. Right. Just call him." I pulled out my phone and locked myself in the bathroom so he wouldn't hear the music or the people and ruin the surprise. It rang and rang and then his voicemail kicked in. "Hi, Trev. Just wondering if everything is all right? I thought we were supposed to meet at my place at eight. Call me."

All of his friends and the guys from Search and Rescue shot awkward glances at me when I returned to the living room. To avoid their stares I ducked back into the kitchen and updated Sophie. "He didn't answer," I mumbled.

Sophie didn't say anything and I could tell by her silence that she didn't think it was good.

Trevor's dad wandered into the kitchen and ate a few chicken wings before he realized there was tension. "What's going on?"

"Trevor was supposed to be here at eight and he isn't answering his phone," I said.

Jim grabbed another chicken wing. "He'll be here." He piled a few other appetizers on a plate, then went back into the living room. When he sat back down, he leaned over to say something to Murphy. Murphy nodded and then got off the couch, walked towards the hallway, and pulled his phone out of his pocket. He rested up against the wall with his enormous back to me. Less than a minute later, he went back to sit beside Jim on the couch and whispered something. They both turned to look at me. When they saw that I was staring at them they both forced smiles before they turned back and pretended to watch the game.

By nine-fifteen, more people started asking when Trevor was supposed to be arriving. By nine-forty-five, they made polite excuses for why they needed to get back up to Squamish. By ten o'clock, the only people left were my mom, my granddad, Jim, Kailyn, Sophie, and Murphy.

"Why didn't Trevor come to his own surprise party?" Kailyn asked her dad in a heartbreaking way.

"I don't know, Kiki. Something must have come up." He patted her shoulder in a reassuring way, even though his expression didn't sell it.

There was a long, heavy silence as they all either stared at the floor or fidgeted with whatever happened to be within reach. "I'm sure he's fine," Sophie finally said and hugged me.

"I had a vision this morning," I blurted out. The words dropped like a grenade. Everyone except Kailyn turned at the same time and stared at me. "In the vision, I couldn't find him. He was lost and I was calling his name, but he didn't answer. I'm scared it means something bad has happened."

They shot uneasy glances at each other. Ever since I was a kid I'd experienced intuitive visions. I hadn't had many since I moved away from Britannia Beach, but the ones I did have were very accurate and gave me warning before things like a pop quiz in my lab and when my granddad fell from a ladder in his condo in Squamish. Unfortunately, I didn't see that one quite early enough to warn him and prevent him from getting a concussion, but luckily I sent Sophie over to check on him. She found him on the floor and took him to the hospital.

I had assumed the vision I'd had in the morning was a mixed signal or symbolic of something else because Trevor never got lost. He found people who were lost. It still didn't make sense, but the fact that he was not where he was supposed to be was a very bad sign.

Sophie dropped dishes into the sink of soapy water and scrubbed vigorously. Murphy left the room, probably to call Trevor again. He returned only a minute later and shook his head at Jim, which made my mom walk out of the kitchen. She sat down in an armchair and stared out the floor-to-ceiling window. Her hand shook as she pressed it to her mouth.

"Maybe he's studying and lost track of time. Or, I bet he fell asleep," Sophie offered. "Doug missed a gig once because he fell asleep. The band tried to get a hold of him, but he'd turned the ringer off on his phone."

"You're probably right." I checked my phone again to see if I had missed a text. "You guys can head back to Squamish. I'll go by his dorm to make sure he's okay."

Sophie put her coat on. Jim looked as if he didn't want to leave, but it was getting late and they still had to drive back to

Britannia Beach. "I'll take Kailyn with me," Jim said to Murphy. "Thanks for bringing her down."

"No problem. I'll go by the dorm with Derian and call you later," Murphy said.

Everyone except Murphy left. I rushed to my room and changed into yoga pants and a sweatshirt, then grabbed my purse. Mom was still sitting in the armchair staring out the window with a distant look on her face. It was the expression she got whenever she was thinking about my dad and the accident. "I'll call you when we find him," I said as I took long strides through the living room and met Murphy at the door. It was hard to tell if she heard me. She didn't move.

Murphy and I didn't talk as we waited for the elevator, or as we walked to his old green GMC pick-up truck that was parked on the street in front of the building. He opened the door for me, then walked around the back to get in the driver's side. The truck shocks shifted and squeaked from his weight.

"Do you think he fell asleep?" I asked as we headed to the university.

He took a deep breath. "Probably."

"What else could have happened?"

"Lots of things. I'm sure he's fine, though." His fingers tightened around the steering wheel, making his knuckles turn white.

"The hospital would have contacted Jim by now if he was in an accident. Right?"

"Probably. I'm sure he's fine."

I looked at Murphy and bit my bottom lip to make it stop trembling.

"What?" he asked.

"It's just as upsetting if he's fine. It means he forgot about me and didn't even call to make up an excuse for why he bailed on our date."

"I'm sure he's fine, and I'm sure he didn't just forget about you. He has worshipped you our entire lives."

"Then where the hell is he?"

He shook his head and seemed to seriously consider the possibilities before he answered, "I don't know."

I turned to look out the passenger side window and went over in my mind the conversation that Trevor and I'd had the evening before. "It's my fault. I scheduled it two weeks before his real birthday so he wouldn't suspect anything and then I was too evasive with the plans for tonight. Maybe we had a miscommunication. He probably thought I meant come by if he had time. He's been really busy lately. I should have told him all of his friends and family were coming down for a party." I shook my head and sighed. "The surprise was definitely a bad idea."

We parked on the south side of the campus and walked along the sidewalk to the dorms. When we entered Trevor's building, I led the way in front of Murphy down the hallway because his massive frame took up almost the entire width of the corridor. I had to take a few deep breaths to prepare myself for heartbreaking news before I lifted my hand and knocked on the door to his room. There was movement inside and then the door opened. It was his roommate. "Hi, Derian. What's up?"

"Hi, Nick. Is Trevor here?"

"No. I thought he was going over to your place." He looked over my shoulder at my hulking, bald bodyguard.

"Oh, sorry. This is Trevor's best friend, Murphy. Murph, this is Trevor's room-mate, Nick." They shook hands. "Trevor was supposed to come over, but he didn't show up and he's not answering his phone."

"Hmm. That's not like him. I haven't seen him since this morning. I think he planned to study with some classmates at the library this afternoon, but it's probably closed now."

I already knew that much, so I hid my disappointment with a forced smile. "Okay, thanks." I glanced into the room that was only big enough for two desks, two beds, and the one closet that they shared. Who knows why I felt the need to see for myself?

He wasn't going to appear out of thin air. "If you see him will you please ask him to give me a call?"

"Yeah, of course. I'll text a couple of our buddies too. Maybe I can track him down."

"Thanks, Nick. We'll just be walking around campus to see if we run into him."

"Okay. Good luck."

Nick closed the door and my phone buzzed with a text from a number I didn't recognize: *Dealing with something serious. Will call when I can.*

My heart pounded with dread as I held up my phone for Murphy to read the message. "Do you think it's from Trevor? It must be. Why isn't he using his own phone? What does he mean by 'serious'? It's kind of cryptic. That's weird, right?"

Murphy raised his eyebrow in a way that upset me. He didn't say anything. He didn't have to because the deep crease that formed between his eyebrows, and the fact that he wouldn't look me directly in the eyes, told me he was concerned. I typed a reply, asking for more details, but got no response.

Chapter 2

Murphy and I rushed down the path that led to the centre of campus. Huge cedar and fir trees lined the walkway and it was dimly lit, so I was extra glad Murphy was with me. I didn't know if Trevor had meant personally serious like depression and suicidal thoughts, or medically serious like heart pains and broken bones, or mechanically serious like a basement flood, or academically serious like quantum physics. The possibilities were endless.

With nothing to go on, we checked the library Trevor and I both usually studied at first. It was closed. Sometimes he studied in a student lounge, which was open twenty-four hours, but he wasn't there either. The campus was essentially a small city with restaurants and coffee shops spread throughout the streets. It would be impossible to check them all, so I focused on places where he hung out the most.

"Maybe we should check the pubs," Murphy suggested.

Even though the thought of Trevor being at a pub instead of on an agreed-upon date with me hurt my feelings, it was the next probable place he would have gone on a Friday night, but still not likely a place where he'd be dealing with something serious. Unless it was a bar fight. We crossed the campus towards the Irish pub he liked the best.

He wasn't at the pub so we circled around by the football field and then headed back in the direction of his dorm. About one hundred metres down the dark path, a couple walked towards us. I could only make out their silhouettes and I wouldn't have thought much of it if I hadn't recognized the outline of Trevor's broad shoulders. I stopped walking and stood frozen in the middle of the path as they approached. Murphy didn't seem to realize it was Trevor, but as they got closer, we heard his voice. The girl laughed as if she'd been drinking. My heart contorted into some sort of seizure and slammed against my lungs, which pushed all the air out. I couldn't make the breath suck back in.

She was the something serious he was dealing with? Seriously?

Murphy reached over and wrapped his arm around my waist to hold me up. Somehow he knew before I did that my knees were just about to get weak from the shock of seeing Trevor with someone else. My eyeballs burned because I hadn't blinked since I first spotted them. The girl stumbled sideways and had to place one hand down on the ground to steady herself. Trevor attempted to prevent her from falling but she landed on the grass and pulled him as if she wanted him to topple down on top of her. He caught his balance in time and said something to her that I couldn't quite hear.

I turned around, twisted out of Murphy's arms, and hurried down the path away from them.

"Wait," Murphy called after me.

"I've seen enough, thanks."

"Murphy?" Trevor shouted, and seemed relieved to see him.

"Is that your friend?" the girl asked. "He's gigantic." She laughed. "That's a funny word—ji-gan-tic, guy-jant-tic. Say it. It sounds funny."

"Deri," Trevor called as I walked away. I didn't want to know why he was stumbling around at midnight with a drunk girl, so I kept going.

Murphy ran after me, caught my elbow, and turned me towards

him. He leaned in closely and said, "Let me talk to him. Just wait here."

"I can't watch," I said and fought to hold back tears.

"You don't even know what's going on. I'm going to talk to him. Don't go anywhere."

"Give me the keys. I'll wait in the truck. And his explanation better be really good."

Murphy handed me the keys and turned to go back to where Trevor was helping the woman to her feet as she sang off-key. I hurried back to the parking lot, climbed into the truck, and stared out the window dumbfounded. I thought things had been good between Trevor and me. As far as I knew, everything was great. I was so in love. I would have sworn he was too. I was glad he wasn't lying dead in a ditch somewhere. But it was completely shattering that he would blow me off to get drunk with some other girl. And then lie about it. It was shocking. It was devastating. It was so not like him.

Maybe things between us hadn't been as good as I thought. Maybe I wasn't putting enough effort into the relationship, or maybe I was a disappointment to him. Did our relationship go from inseparable as children into teenage sweethearts and then slip into the someone-I-used-to-know category without me noticing? Maybe adulthood changed us. It was possible that after waiting thirteen years to date his life-long crush, when it actually happened, I was a colossal let-down. I didn't feel that way about him. In fact, dating the guy who was not only an amazing friend but also someone I had dreamed of being with for years had turned out to be a million times better than I had even imagined it would be.

It was my fault the relationship had unraveled. I hadn't been spending enough time with him. My course load was ridiculously heavy. And even when we did have some spare time between studying, with me being at my mom's and him having a roommate, we barely had enough privacy to even make out. Maybe he compared us to Sophie and Doug, who had plans to move in together. Or to Murphy and Rene, who already lived together and were ready to start a family. I wasn't ready for that. Maybe Trevor was.

I winced when I realized that's what my vision was about. I lost him.

The truck door opened, but I didn't look over because I already knew it was Murphy, not Trevor. "He's just walking her home. He'll be right back to talk to you."

I shook my head and mumbled, "I'm tired. I just want to go home."

"You need to give him a chance to explain, Deri. A situation came up and he didn't feel she was in a state to get home safely by herself."

"I'm really tired and upset. Just call him and tell him I'll talk to him in the morning."

"I can't. He lost his phone somewhere."

"Convenient," I mumbled.

Murphy shot me a grow-up-Deri expression. "He's walking her home so she'll be safe. You know that."

Obviously it was more in character for Trevor to get involved in a situation where someone in trouble needed help rather than blow off plans with me to hang out with some random chick. I knew that, but I also had to face the possibility that I wasn't cutting it in the girlfriend department. It was late and I was already being snappy and rude due to the lack of sleep from earlier in the week. I was afraid I would make everything worse if I tried to talk about it when I was so exhausted and emotional. "I just want to go home. Please."

Murphy sighed and then reluctantly started the truck. He was quiet for most of the drive, then he said, "I know that looked bad, but he's a good guy, Derian—you know that. And I've known him for almost fourteen years; he would never cheat on you. He was just helping someone who got caught up in a dangerous situation. That's all."

"Maybe I did something to push him away, or maybe he wanted something new," I said as he turned out onto the street.

"He wants you, Deri. Trust me. He waited until you graduated to ask you out, but he wanted to date you for at least three years before that. And he's loved you since the day he moved to Britannia Beach. He wouldn't do anything to disrespect you or screw up what you guys have. If I could get him to stop constantly talking about how great you are, I would." He smiled as he reached across the cab of the truck and shoved my shoulder. "I'm sick of it, frankly."

It did make me feel better to hear Murphy say that, but then the image of Trevor and the woman catapulted me right back into a sludgy pool of self-doubt. "Did he seem unhappy about our relationship lately?"

"No. A bond like what you two have always had doesn't just disappear. He's been stressed out with school and coming up to Britannia Beach for rescues on weekends. But he has never said anything negative about you or the relationship. In fact, when he talks about the future, you are always included in that conversation. There is no doubt in his mind what he wants."

It was true. Trevor never came across as unsure or as losing interest. He had been working really hard at school and still volunteering for Search and Rescue. That girl was definitely too drunk to safely walk home alone. It was most likely all innocent, but because of my vision about losing Trevor, I couldn't help obsessing about the things I could have done to be a better girlfriend and a better friend to him. I should have never taken what we had for granted. I should have seen the signs that he was drifting away.

Or maybe he wasn't. In his defence, he didn't know about the party. If everybody hadn't been at the condo waiting it wouldn't have even been that big of a deal that he didn't show up. But the vision bothered me. It was trying to warn me that I was losing him. And if that was true, the girl was potentially more than just someone he walked home. Or she might be, at some point in the future. It was an omen. Or not. I didn't know what to think. And it was giving me a headache.

When Murphy pulled up in front of my mom's condo, I opened the door and climbed out of the truck. "Thanks for the ride. Be safe driving home."

"Just hear him out."

I nodded. "I will. Good night, Murph. Thanks for everything. Don't forget to call his dad. I don't want him to worry."

I took the elevator upstairs and stood in the hall. I was hesitant to go in because I didn't want to deal with a million questions from my mom. I couldn't avoid it forever, though, so I finally decided to plaster a smile across my face and act as if I was totally relieved. My plan was to lie and tell her that he just fell asleep. I opened the door, expecting to see her still sitting in the armchair. Fortunately, it looked as if she'd gone to bed and left one lamp on in the hallway for me.

I got ready for bed as quickly as I could and dove under my sheets in case she got up and asked me what happened. Only a second after I clicked my lamp off there was a knock on my door. She opened it a crack and poked her head in. I cringed.

"Everything okay?"

"Yeah. Everybody is safe and sound. Good night."

I could sense her lingering. But she didn't say anything else before she eventually closed the door. My phone buzzed with a text so I rolled over and reached towards my bedside table. The phone number wasn't familiar.

Always in my heart

Trevor had obviously borrowed someone's phone, which was sweet. But I got sad at the thought that it might be hers. It was probably Nick's, but I was still hurt by the possibility that it could have been hers. I replied *Love You* and then thought about how I was going to fix things as I twisted the ring he gave me around my finger.

Chapter 3

In the morning, the light peeked through my curtains and brightened the ceiling patterns that I had been staring at all night. It took every ounce of energy I had to slump out of bed and cross the hall to the bathroom. When I saw my face in the mirror, I actually gasped. The rims of my eyelids were blood-red and the dark circles under my eyes made me look like a desiccated vampire.

I stood in the shower and waited for the water to warm me up. I almost didn't have the motivation to get back out, but my legs were tired of holding me up, so I turned the water off and put a robe on. I didn't even dry my hair before I shuffled down the hall towards the kitchen to boil water for tea. Trevor was seated at the kitchen bar. He looked a million times worse than I did.

"Morning, sunshine," he said hoarsely.

I didn't respond, partly because I was surprised to see him and partly because I didn't know where to start. My mom had obviously let him in on her way out and I wondered what he had told her. His dark hair stuck up in different directions and he was wearing the same thing he'd had on the night before. The rock from Britannia Beach that I'd had engraved with the *Always*

In My Heart inscription for him was in his hands. He cradled it in his palm as if it were an injured bird. "Thanks for the birthday present. I love it."

My eyebrows angled together and I walked to the sink to fill the kettle. I was apparently still not in the right frame of mind to sort everything out. I placed the kettle on the stove. I could feel him staring at me as I dropped tea bags in two mugs and waited for the water to boil.

"Deri." The sound of his voice made my heart ache. "Derian," he whispered, so softly.

It felt like he wanted to deliver bad news to me. Like break-up kind of bad. I didn't want to admit that everything I had always wanted was over, but maybe it was impossible for a special childhood friendship that turned into an intense adolescent love to last forever. It felt as if my heart was being peeled into shreds one thin layer at a time. It was excruciating.

"Murphy said you planned a surprise." He waited for me to respond, but I was too choked up to speak. When I didn't say anything he exhaled heavily. "I'm so sorry I missed it."

I looked over my shoulder at him. "Were you out with that woman?"

"No. I was studying with a couple of friends from class all afternoon and we went to the pub for a pint. When I realized it was almost eight, I'd had a few drinks and didn't think it was a good idea to drive, so I headed over to catch the bus. I would have called, but I don't know where my phone is. I think it was stolen at the library or fell out of my pocket." He stopped talking and stood, inching only slightly closer, as if he wasn't sure how to gauge my mood.

I folded my arms across my chest and leaned my butt against the counter. "What happened between going to the bus and Murphy and me finding you with that woman almost four hours later?"

"I ran into Ethan, the guy in my biology class; you met him

at that Halloween party, he was dressed as Muhammad Ali."

I nodded, not because I remembered Ethan, but because I wanted him to get on with the story.

"Ethan's girlfriend, Abbi, had texted him saying that she was worried about one of her friends because she couldn't find her. They belong to a sorority that had a dinner party and it got crashed by a bunch of frat guys who turned it into a kegger. The last time Abbi had seen her friend, she'd been dancing with some guy nobody knew and then they disappeared. Ethan and I headed over to the sorority house to help Abbi look for her. It took a while, but we eventually found her in a laneway, unconscious."

"Oh my God. Is she okay?"

He shook his head and his forehead creased with stress. "She'd been drugged and her clothes were torn."

An awful feeling weighed heavy in my stomach, partly because she'd been assaulted and partly because I had been so selfishly worried about something that suddenly seemed so trivial. "That's horrible. Did they catch the guy?"

"They will. The police questioned everyone after the ambulance left and they know who did it; they're going to pull surveillance first to make sure the case sticks."

"Was that Abbi you were walking home?"

"A friend of hers. She asked me if I'd walk her home because she'd had too much to drink. I texted you from Ethan's phone to tell you there had been an emergency. Didn't you get it?"

"I did, and at first I was sick with worry, but then we found you and I thought you had lied so you could hang out with someone else." The kettle started to scream. I turned around and poured water into the mugs.

"Why would I lie?"

"I don't know. I feel like an idiot for assuming that you were with her in a romantic way. I'm so sorry I didn't stay and give you a chance to explain."

Trevor's arms wrapped around my waist from behind. He hugged me and rested his chin on my shoulder. I could hear the smile in his voice as he said, "I can't believe you doubted my feelings for you."

"I was afraid you changed your mind."

"That will never happen." He kissed my neck. "From the day I met you, all I wanted was to be near you. And if I'm not here right by your side, guaranteed it's because something really bad has happened."

I turned and reached up to touch his face, a face I'd known most of my life. "Don't even say that. I don't ever want to lose you."

"You won't. You're the best thing in my life. You always have been and you always will be. I will be yours forever, if you want me."

I leaned in and kissed him. "You are what I have always wanted and what I will always want."

He smiled and tipped his head forward until our foreheads rested on each other.

"I'm sorry I overreacted, and jumped to crazy, unwarranted conclusions, and acted embarrassingly selfish and jealous when you were doing a great thing and helping someone who was in danger. I've been really stressed and tired and I had a vision that scared me, so I'm definitely too sensitive right now."

"What was your vision about?"

"I'm not sure. It was vague. I couldn't find you. Or, maybe you couldn't find me. It didn't make any sense, but it scared me. I thought it was an omen."

"I will always find you." His hand slid up to cradle the back of my neck. "No matter where you are; I will always find you."

"I know." I kissed him. "That's one of the things I love about you. And you're hot body is another thing." I tickled his ribs as my eyebrows rose suggestively. "My mom's out with Ron if you want to hang out for a while."

He caught the hint and picked me up to carry me to my room.

"Are you going to make me breakfast afterwards?"

"Of course."

"With apple-cinnamon muffins?"

"Of course."

He smiled and then kicked my bedroom door shut behind us.

Chapter 4

I woke up late the next morning and rushed to pack my bag to spend reading week with Sophie in Tofino—rain gear, toques, scarves, gloves, long johns, rubber boots, wool sweaters, and all my textbooks. The weather forecast was for torrential rain and cold temperatures. I had only been to Sophie's cousin's cabin on the west coast of Vancouver Island one other time and it was during the summer. I kind of remembered it being really windy and cold even in the middle of August, so I packed as many warm clothes as I could fit in my bag.

Sophie showed up at eight in the morning, grinning with her hand propped on her hip—she was never in a good mood in the morning. Something weird was definitely up. She was wearing tiny jean shorts, a t-shirt, and flip flops.

"Uh, why are you chipper this early and why are you dressed like that?"

"Change of plans."

"Changed how?"

She pulled all of the warm clothes out of my bag. "You're not going to need these."

"What? Why?"

She jumped up and down and waved two pieces of paper in

front of my face. "My dad got us stand-by tickets to Acapulco and booked us in at an all-inclusive resort."

I shook my head to make the information sink in. "Are you kidding?"

"Nope. I already asked your mom and she's cool with it."

Not sure if I was more shocked about the tickets to Acapulco or the fact my mom agreed, I paused. "Seriously?"

"My dad is convinced I need to travel, meet people, and experience other cultures. Date other guys."

"But your parents like Doug."

She shrugged and took a while to answer. "They don't like that I've only dated one guy since I was fourteen. And they're really not thrilled that he wants me to move to LA. Whatever, it's a good time for me to travel and maybe figure out what I want to do with my life. We're going to Mexico for a week—all expenses paid."

"Shut up!" I squealed and jumped up and down with her. Then my heart sank when it hit me that I couldn't go. "I have way too much studying to do."

"Study, schmudy. You can read on the plane, on the beach, by the pool. Would you rather read textbooks in the freezing-cold Tofino rain or in the decadently warm Acapulco sunshine?"

"Good point." I didn't even need convincing. "Sunshine, here we come. Yes." I did a fist-pump and leapt around my room to dump all the winter clothes into my closet. I filled a suitcase with shorts, bathing suits, summer dresses, hats, sunglasses, and sandals.

"Don't forget club outfits," Sophie hollered from the living room.

I grabbed some dressy clothes from my closet and opened the drawer to my bedside table to pull out the box Mason's necklace was in. It was the nicest thing I owned and it would be one of the few times I could wear it without Trevor knowing.

"Mom!" I shouted and spun around, startled because she was already standing in the doorway, smiling.

"Are you really okay with us going to Mexico?"

"Yes. I think it will be a great experience. You've been working too hard at school lately and the stress has been getting to you. Here's your passport."

"Thanks." I gave her a big hug. "This is so awesome. I have to tell Trevor." When he didn't respond to the text, I remembered that his phone was still lost. I hoped we had time to go by and see him before the flight. I skipped out into the living room and danced around with Sophie like hyper cheerleaders for another few seconds before we said goodbye to my mom and hurried down to Sophie's car. "We have to stop by UBC on the way to the airport."

"Yeah, I figured. So where was he the other night? You kind of left out all the juicy details when you texted to say you found him."

"There was an emergency at school and he had to help a friend."

"What kind of emergency?"

"A girl was drugged and date-raped. They helped find her and called the ambulance and police."

"Jesus. Is it weird that I'm totally not surprised that's the reason he no-showed? I hope they caught the piece of shit who did it."

"Yeah, apparently someone at the party knew who he was. So that's good."

"It's great. And you know what else is great? We're going to Mexi-cooo," she sang.

"Woo!"

We parked on campus and ran to Trevor's building. We were laughing and holding hands like we used to when we were little girls. A classmate of Trevor's named Beth—tall, with long, wavy, brown hair and a pin-up girl figure—was at the front door and just about to go into the building. I had met her at least six times before because she often sat with Trevor's friends for lunch and she went to two football games with a whole group of us, but she always acted like she had no idea I was Trevor's girlfriend.

She turned to hold the door open for us, then smiled. "Derian, right?"

I nodded, surprised that she actually remembered my name.

"I was just going up to see Trevor. I found his phone on the floor in my room. He must have left it there the other night."

Sophie whimpered a little as I dug my fingers into her hand.

"Here." Beth held the phone out. "Would you be a sweetie and give it to him for me?"

I didn't move to get the phone. Sophie finally extended her free arm and took the phone from Beth.

"Thanks. Tell Trev that I'll see him tonight at study group. It was nice seeing you again." Her smile was so phoney I wanted to puke.

"Okay, ow! You can release the vice on my hand now," Sophie complained after Beth strutted away.

I stormed into Trevor's building. Sophie chased after me. I pounded on his door with unnecessary force. When he opened the door, he was grinning, but when he saw my expression, his smile faded. "What's wrong?"

I held my palm up to signal Sophie to produce the phone. "We ran into Beth downstairs. She was kind enough to return your phone."

"Where did she find it?"

"On the floor in her bedroom, apparently. She said you must have left it there the other night."

"What?" He frowned as the information sunk in. "I've never been in her room. I don't even know which apartment she lives in. Did she really say I was in her room?"

"She certainly did." I passed the phone to him. "I came by to tell you that Sophie and I are going to Mexico for a week instead of Tofino. Have fun at study group tonight." I spun around and took long, fast strides down the hall. When I realized Sophie hadn't followed me I turned back to give her a "come on" gesture. She and Trevor were both standing in front of his door staring at me.

"Derian, you can't leave things like that," Sophie called. "That

whore was lying. Trust me, I know a lying whore when I see one."
She walked towards me, stood close, and whispered, "Don't let a
girl like that weasel her way in and ruin what you guys have. I'll
wait in the car. Take your time."

After Sophie left, I stood in the hall staring at the tiles. I didn't
actually look, but I could feel Trevor waiting patiently. I was going
to be gone for a week and I didn't want things to be bad between
us. I wouldn't be able to relax if I knew that the last thing I said
to him was hostile. I thought about what Sophie said. She had
to handle groupies hitting on Doug all the time and she was right
that I shouldn't believe Beth over Trevor. When I eventually looked
up at him, he smiled, probably because he knew I wouldn't leave
still mad at him.

He walked over to hug me. "She's lying."

I rested my cheek on his chest and listened to the comforting
rhythm of his heart beat. "I know. But why would she lie?"

"I don't know. She's obviously trying to break us up."

Lying or not lying, that part was definitely true. There were
so many things testing our bond. I didn't want it to break.

"The last time I remember having my phone was when I was
at the library. She must have taken it." He leaned back and held
my face between his palms. "I won't study with her anymore."

The sincerity in his eyes reassured me completely. We were
unbreakable. The universe could throw as many tests as it wanted
at us. "I don't want you to mess up your grades. If you have to
work in a group with her I trust you." I leaned forward and
kissed him.

He pressed me against the wall and his hands slid down the
side of my body to rest on my hips. "Are you really going to
Mexico instead of Tofino?"

"Yeah, Sophie's dad gave us stand-by tickets with his airline
and he's paying for an all-inclusive resort. Here's where we're
staying." I handed him the piece of paper that I had written the
hotel information on. "I'll email you every day."

He leaned in and whispered, "I don't want you to go away," before he kissed his way down my neck.

I leaned my head back and closed my eyes, enjoying the soft touch of his lips against my skin. "I don't want to go away anymore," I whispered back and clutched his hair to draw his lips to mine.

"Hi, Derian," Nick said loudly to interrupt our make-out session as he walked up. "Nice to see you again." He paused and leaned in close to us, grinning. "How's it going?" Trevor laughed and shoved him in the shoulder. "Oh, are you guys busy? My bad." He mussed Trevor's hair before carrying on towards their room "Don't let me interrupt. We can talk later." Before he disappeared through the doorway he pointed at us and made his eyebrows dance in an animated way.

Once we were alone again I kissed Trevor softly and whispered, "I love you so much." I touched his chest. "Always in my heart."

"I love you, too. Have fun in Mexico, but be safe."

"Always am." I smiled and kissed him one more time. "See ya, Maverty."

"See ya, Lafleur."

Nick poked his head back out into the hall. "Bye, Derian."

"Bye, Nick." I kissed my fingertips and blew it towards Trevor. Nick pretended to catch it, which earned him a body-slam into the wall.

"Okay, I give up," Nick choked out.

Trevor let him go and they both stood grinning at me. I shook my head and waved before I took the stairs two at a time. I jogged to the car and flung the door open, which startled Sophie. "Sorry I took so long," I said breathlessly.

"Was it worth it?"

"Definitely."

"All right, Mexico, here we come."

"Wooo!"

Chapter 5

I was too excited to read my textbook as Sophie and I waited at the airport gate to see if we could get on the next flight. I people-watched and made up stories in my head about why they were travelling. A young guy kept looking at a picture in his hand and smiling longingly, so I decided he was flying to meet a woman he met online. A woman whose eyes were red as if she had been crying typed on her phone the entire time she waited. I decided she was the oldest sibling and her father had died, so she was trying to arrange everything for the funeral. I also saw a family with two little boys. They looked like twins, but one had no hair and his skin was pale. He seemed weak and leaned his head on his mom's shoulder. The healthy-looking one stood at the windows with his dad and pointed at an airplane that was taking off. I decided they were going to their grandparents' cabin because it was the sick one's dying wish. It reminded me of Mason and his twin brother. Cody had died of cancer the same year my dad died. Mason's mom once told me that Cody's dying wish had been to go fishing at their grandparents' cabin, and seeing the boys in the airport made my eyes tear up.

"What the hell?" Sophie asked when she noticed I was getting choked up.

"I was just thinking about something sad."

She was about to ask me what it was when her dad walked up to us. He looked handsome in his pilot's uniform. "Hi, Dad." She stood and hugged him.

"Are you girls all ready for some fun in the sun?"

"Yes. Thank you so much for the tickets, Mr. Sakamoto."

"You're welcome. Make sure you stay close to the resort. There have been some travel alerts for some of the surrounding areas." The loud speaker announced our names and asked us to go up to the front counter. "Sounds like there's room on this flight. I better get to my gate too. I'm off to snowy Montreal." He hugged us both and warned, "Be safe."

"We will. Love you, Dad."

Sophie and I skipped up to the counter and got our boarding passes for the last two seats on the flight. Once we were boarded and settled, Sophie stuck her ear buds in and flipped through a magazine. I took a textbook out of my carry-on and placed it on my lap. As I watched the ground crew load up the last of the luggage, I had a vision. I was on my knees praying for Trevor. Then it ended. That was it. Weird.

Sophie pulled out one of her ear buds. "Everything okay?"

"Yeah." I turned to stare out the window again.

"What did you see?"

"Nothing that makes any sense, since I'm not even religious."

"If you saw the plane crashing, you should tell me now."

"I don't think that's what it was."

"You don't think? Great." She moaned and put her ear bud back in.

It was insanely hot in Acapulco. My jeans stuck to my legs the minute we stepped off the plane. If I had spotted a pair of scissors I would have cut them into shorts right there in the airport. I didn't see any scissors lying around, but fortunately the shuttle to the resort was air-conditioned.

The five-star resort was massive and gorgeous. It had four

restaurants, six pools, a nightclub, a bar every twenty feet, and it was right on the beach. I could hear the waves crashing from the open-air lobby. Sophie threw around tips to the shuttle driver, the older man who handed us a cocktail as we arrived, and the cute guy who carried our bags to our room. "*Gracias* Miss Sagamomo," he attempted her name.

"Call me Sophie."

"*Gracias* Miss Sophie." He smiled a big, white, toothy smile.

"What's your name?"

He pointed to the nametag on his chest. "Luis. If you need anything, Miss Sophie, just ask for Luis."

"*Gracias*, Luis."

The suite was sprawling and the bedroom was separated from the living room by double doors. I opened the sliding patio door and stepped out onto the balcony. It over-looked the pools below and the ocean beyond that. I closed my eyes and let the sun and the warm ocean breeze soak into my skin. It was amazing—like what paradise was supposed to feel like. The only thing better would have been being there with Trevor too.

My thoughts were interrupted when a male voice said, "Hi." A tanned guy with longish blond hair and green eyes was standing on the balcony next to ours. He leaned on the railing with one hand and drank from a red plastic cup with his other hand. He smelled like a mix of coconut suntan lotion and alcohol.

"Hi," I replied.

"Did you just get here?"

"What gave it away—the pasty skin or the jeans?"

"Neither, I just would have noticed you before now if you'd been here the whole time. I'm Liam."

"Derian." I reached across the gap between our balconies and shook his hand. "Have you been here long?"

"Three days. I should probably apologize in advance because my friends are a little loud and can be obnoxious. Well, not can be; they are obnoxious."

"But you're not?"

"Oh, I am too. I apologize for that in advance as well."

I laughed. "Where are you from?"

"Toronto. It's in Canada."

"Really? Is it true that you live in igloos in Canada?" I teased.

He looked at me to see if I was dumb or joking. He smiled. "You're Canadian too, aren't you?"

"Vancouver."

"I should have known that." He turned his head a little when a guy's voice called him from inside the room. He looked back at me. "We're just heading out to get some dinner. Do you and your friends want to come with us?"

"It's just my friend Sophie and me, and we kind of want to freshen up first. Maybe we'll see you down there later."

"I'll buy you a drink," he joked.

"Ha ha, big spender."

Sophie stepped out onto the balcony behind me and rested her elbow on my shoulder. "What do we have here?"

"Sophie, Liam. Liam, Sophie."

He reached over to shake her hand. He grinned in a very mischievous way and said, "You two are going to get into all sorts of trouble here. Hopefully we'll run into you down at the club." He waved and went back into his room.

"Cuuuute," Sophie purred.

"Not as cute as Doug," I reminded her.

"Yeah, yeah. Let's get ready."

I showered, then Sophie straightened my hair. She always made it look so smooth and shiny. I loved it. I dressed in a fitted, white sundress and did my makeup. Sophie put on classy black shorts that had a cuff at the hem, and a silky green backless top that scooped low and kind of billowed at the front. She straightened her bangs into a perfectly level line across her forehead and layered on a couple of chains that shimmered on her skin. She made fashion look so effortless. I clasped on the necklace that Mason gave me and slipped into a pair of strappy heels.

We decided to try the Italian restaurant. As we walked through the lobby, I noticed there were computer stations, so I stopped and emailed Trevor.

We made it safe and sound. The resort is beautiful, but I wish you and Doug were here with us. Going for dinner now. Love u. D.

The dinner was awesome and we ate way too much because the idea of it being pre-paid made us gluttonous. We each had a margarita with dinner. It went straight to my head because the only alcohol I'd ever had was a glass of champagne at my cousin's wedding and the cocktail that the hotel gave us when we arrived. Apparently, alcohol made me giggly, because I couldn't stop laughing.

We eventually made our way over to the nightclub. It was packed with college students, who were all obviously desperately in need of reading break. There were no available tables, so we stood next to the bar and had another margarita. My legs started to get tingly.

"Hey, you made it." Liam draped his arm across my shoulders.

I giggled.

"Sophie, this is my wing-man, Ben," Liam said.

Sophie smiled at the tall guy, who looked half-Asian and half-Caucasian. "Hi, Ben."

"Do you want to dance?" Liam asked me.

"I'll try. I can't exactly feel my legs."

"You're a lightweight, eh?"

"You could say that."

He led me by the hand towards the dance floor, then wrapped his arms around my waist. I propped my hands on his shoulders, mostly to hold myself up. "You look beautiful," he said.

"Thanks. I have a boyfriend. You should probably know that."

"I know." He held my hand above my head to twirl me around.

"How do you know?"

"Because girls like you always have boyfriends. Don't worry about it. We're just dancing."

"Yeah, just dancing."

Liam and I alternated between dancing and hanging out with Sophie and Ben. It was fun. I thought the boys said they were students at the University of Toronto, but that might not have been what they said because when I said, "I considered going to U of T," they all laughed at me as if it didn't make sense.

"Is the music getting louder?" I shouted.

Liam chuckled. "No, you're just getting drunker."

"I love this song. Let's dance." I dragged him back out onto the dance floor. He wasn't a very good dancer. He mostly just positioned his hands on my waist or hips and watched as I danced. After another margarita, my eyesight started to get a little blurry. I could sort of see Sophie. She was smiling and she looked completely sober as she talked to Ben.

Some other guy handed me a drink and I was just about to drink it when Sophie grabbed it and took it away from me. "Nice try," she yelled at the guy. "Derian, don't take drinks unless they're from the bar. In fact, don't take any more drinks at all."

I saluted her and stumbled back out onto the dance floor. Not much of anything was clear after that. Ben and Liam walked us back to the room. Well, they walked and Liam carried me over his shoulder.

The next thing I remembered clearly was waking up in the morning with a crushing pressure clamping down on my head. The sun streamed through the window and felt like someone turned the brightness up too high. I ran to the bathroom and wasn't able to lift the toilet in time, so unceremoniously hurled in the bathtub. It was a revolting strawberry-pink mess mixed with what I could only imagine were spaghetti noodles. I used the showerhead and washed it down the drain. It was making me feel sick again as I watched it dilute with water. Sophie propped herself against the bathroom doorframe with her arms crossed and watched me.

"Sorry. You're going to have to tip the maid really big," I croaked hoarsely.

"I see that."

"Why do you look perfectly fine?"

"Because I'm not a rookie."

I sat on the edge of the tub and held my head between my palms to keep it from spinning. "Why did you let me do that to myself?"

"You were my entertainment for the night. Talking to that Ben guy was painful. He's like a child in a sexy man's body. I'm going down to the lobby to check my email. Get cleaned up. I want to sit by the pool."

"Okay," I mumbled, then crawled back into bed and pulled the covers over my head.

Chapter 6

I finally dragged myself out of bed just before noon and we went down to sit by the pool. Sophie made trips to the buffet every twenty minutes and returned with trays of fruits or chocolates and pastries. When I saw her eating Jell-O, taquitos, and baby shrimps all off the same plate, my stomach churned painfully. "That's disgusting," I moaned.

"You're missing out. It's such a waste to be at an all-you-can-eat-and-drink resort and not feel like eating or drinking."

"Even if I didn't drink too much last night I wouldn't be eating that combination."

She shrugged and popped a shrimp into her mouth. "Are you up for a salsa lesson?"

"No."

"Water aerobics?"

"No. You go ahead. I'll just stay here and try to get some reading done."

She stood and pulled her linen cover-up off over her head. I watched as she strutted over to the other side of the pool deck for the salsa lesson. Three guys who had been sitting near the dance instructor jumped up and joined the class when they saw Sophie. They did more ass-watching than salsa dancing.

I struggled through a section of psychology without actually retaining much information on monkeys and attachment disorders. My head hurt and I couldn't even take my sunglasses off to apply sunscreen because the sunlight felt like sabres through my eyeballs.

"Can I get you a drink?" a male voice asked from over my shoulder.

I turned to see if he was talking to me. He was a short guy with massive muscles and a nearly life-sized gold crucifix hanging around his neck. He slid his sunglasses down and peered over them at me. "Oh. No thanks. I'm nursing a hangover." I turned my head back to start reading again.

"What's your name?"

I glanced at him as he moved to sit on Sophie's lounge chair. "Derian."

"Gino." He held his hand out to shake mine. Then he pushed his sunglasses back into place and took a sip of his mojito. It felt as if he was staring at my body. "You're beautiful."

"Thank you." I glanced over to see if I could make eye contact with Sophie. The dance lesson was over and I couldn't see where she went. I scanned the pool deck, but didn't see her anywhere.

"What are you reading?"

"Psychology."

"You should take a break." He pointed over his shoulder at the pool. "Let's go for a swim."

"No thanks. I should finish this."

He took my textbook from me and closed it. "That's boring. You're in Mexico and you only live once. Would you like to go for a walk? There are some cool caves just down the beach. I would love to show them to you."

"No thanks." I grabbed my book back.

"You're getting a little burnt. Pass me the sunscreen. I'll do your back."

I looked over at the bar to see if Sophie was getting a drink.

I couldn't see her. "I already have sunscreen on. Thanks."

"My friends and I are staying in the presidential penthouse suite. Do you want to come up and party?"

I pointed to my textbook. "I don't mean to be rude, but I should really get back to reading. Nice meeting you."

He flexed his bloated pecs as if he thought that would mesmerize me into being interested in him. It didn't impress me. I turned my head to see if Sophie was maybe on her way back from the buffet. She was standing right beside me. She smiled and leaned over to kiss me on the lips. "Hey, babe. Did you miss me?" she asked.

I glanced at Gino. His mouth was frozen in a crooked smile, but his eyebrows were angled in a frown.

"You're on my seat," Sophie said to him. He stood and stared at Sophie as she did a sexy crawl onto the lounge chair. She rolled over and extended her arm over to rest her hand on mine.

Gino tilted his head in a cocky way. "I could be into that."

"No. You couldn't," Sophie snarled. "Go away. You're in my sun."

He shook his head as if he thought she was a bitch, then walked away.

I lifted an eyebrow at her. "Was that necessary?"

"Apparently. I watched you trying your sweet method for like fifteen minutes and he wasn't even close to getting the hint."

"Do you think, when we're forty, you'll still be a menace?"

"Definitely." She stood. "I'm going for a swim. If the vultures start circling, try to be less nice."

She dove in and swam underwater to the other end of the pool. She kicked off the wall and then backstroked towards me. Liam and his friends came running from somewhere behind me and did cannon balls into the pool. They almost landed on Sophie. Ben picked her up and acted as if he was going to launch her, which was an error. She did something to him under the water that made him groan and disappear below the surface. They all laughed.

Liam turned and swam to the edge near where I was. He flattened his hands on the deck and did a push-up to heave himself out of the pool, streaming water over his tanned and fit body. He really was cute. He stood over me to purposely let water drip off his lean muscles onto me. "How are you feeling after last night?"

I pushed his thigh to make him back away and stop dripping on me. "A little better. I won't be doing that again."

"Too bad. It was fun."

"Was it? I don't really recall."

"I didn't leave a lasting impression? Ouch, that hurts." He sat down on Sophie's lounge chair. "Maybe tonight we can hang out again. You can try to show some restraint around the booze and I'll do some charming things that you'll actually remember."

"I have a boyfriend, remember?"

"It's just dancing."

"Right. Just dancing."

"That kiss Sophie gave you to get rid of that guide was kind of hot. It left me with an interesting mental image."

"Keep dreaming."

He stood up abruptly to slide one arm under my knees and one around my back. I squirmed and screamed as he picked me up, took a couple long strides, and leapt into the pool with me in his arms. We hit the water and I heard the splash through the muted watery sound in my ears. I made vicious eye contact with him for a second while we were submerged; he was smiling. I broke the surface before he did and waited for him. As soon as he appeared, I splashed his face, then pushed all my weight down on his head to dunk him. After I held him down long enough to make a point, I swam back to the edge of the pool and got out. The water actually felt great, but I wasn't going to give him the satisfaction of knowing that. I twisted my hair to wring it out, then rubbed a towel across my skin. When I turned back toward the pool, Liam held up my sunglasses, which he had obviously retrieved from the bottom.

"Do you want these?"

"Yes. My retinas are burning."

"Come and get them," he teased.

I walked to the edge and crouched so my chest was in line with his face. "You come here," I said seductively and fluttered my eyelashes.

He frantically treaded closer and his attitude turned serious at the hope that I was flirting with him. He glanced at my chest for a second, then looked back at my face and handed me the glasses. It was so easy.

"Good boy." I patted him on the top of his head and then walked away.

His friends laughed at him. He didn't seem to mind—he shouldn't have minded since he got a close-up peek out of it. Sophie got out of the pool and ran her fingers through her hair. The guys all stood in the pool gawking up at her gorgeous figure. She knew they were drooling, so she bent over and slowly ran the towel up one leg. Then she reached her arms up and twisted her hair into a knot. "Bye, boys," she said before she leaned over to toss her stuff into her bag. I grabbed my bag and followed her.

"Meet us at the club tonight," Liam shouted after us.

We smiled and kept walking. It was fun to mess with them, but they were just goofy boys. I missed Trevor.

My appetite had returned, so I grabbed a plate of fruit from the buffet on the way back up to the room. "How's Doug's tour going?" I asked as I scarfed the food off the plate and she pulled clothes out of the closet.

Sophie glanced at me, then laid out her outfit on the bed. "I don't know."

"I thought you checked your emails earlier."

"I did." She glanced at me again and sighed before she sat on the bed. "I blocked Doug's emails."

"What? Why?"

"Don't freak out, but I broke up with him."

"What?" I bolted up, almost choked on a tortilla-chip shard, and stared at her in complete shock. "When? Why? How come you didn't tell me?"

"Last week. Because we are on completely different paths. You were busy with school and planning the party." She stood and undressed to have a shower. I followed her into the bathroom. She closed the curtain and the water turned on.

"I don't understand. You guys lived on different sides of the continent for six months. Why would you break up with him right before you were supposed to move in with him?"

"He went on a world tour with a band that has hard-core groupies. I'm not cool with being cheated on, so I let him go. Pass me the shampoo from my bag, please."

I handed her the bottle. "How did Doug react?"

"I don't know. I told him right before he got on the plane. He sent me a bunch of messages that I didn't read and then I blocked him."

"Sophie."

She turned the water off and reached out to grab a towel off the rack. I was still standing with my mouth gaped open when she opened the curtain and stepped out. "It was going to end soon anyway. I don't want to talk about it and ruin our holiday. Okay?"

I blinked a few times, trying to process everything. "Yeah. Okay."

Chapter 7

We decided on the French restaurant that was decorated to mimic a Parisian café. I wore a blue, strapless, A-line dress and the same strappy heels as the night before. Sophie wore a black pencil skirt and a spaghetti-strapped, V-neck tank top. Her black pumps had little rock star buckles at the ankle.

I stared at her across the table, not sure what to talk about, given the recent bomb she dropped on me.

"Stop it," she said and pointed a breadstick at me.

"What?"

"I'm not going to talk about Doug."

"I didn't say anything."

"You don't have to. I can tell what you're thinking by that sad puppy-dog look on your face."

The waiter came by with drinks. "No thanks," I said.

"I'll take hers." Sophie motioned with her hand. "Keep them coming."

I watched her down the first drink, then I said, "You guys have been together since you were fourteen. I think you should talk about how you're feeling."

"I'm feeling like I don't want to talk about it."

"Just because Doug is on tour doesn't mean he would cheat."

She tilted her head and glared at me. "You thought Trevor was capable of cheating on you with a whore from school. If you believe that then you must know Doug is capable of cheating with the groupies that follow the band around and throw themselves on him backstage."

The waiter placed our orders on the table. I stared at my plate. Sophie dug in. "I feel like crying," I mumbled.

"I didn't even cry over it." She put a forkful of rich saucy food in her mouth. "This food is unfreakingbelievable."

"You're not normal. You know that, right?"

She laughed. "I've had my suspicions." She waved the waiter over for two more drinks. "Either talk about something other than Doug or don't talk at all."

"Okay," I mumbled and stuffed a forkful of beef in my mouth.

After dessert, Sophie went to the spa reception desk to book us massages for the following afternoon. I went to the lobby to check my email and read Trevor's response to my last one.

I miss you already. It's pouring and cold here. I've been imagining what your body will look like when you come back all tanned. Have fun, I love you.

I wrote back.

Hey Babe, I miss you too. I had too many margaritas last night—rookie mistake. The food is great here. Italian last night, French tonight, maybe Mexican tomorrow night, and a 24-hour buffet. You would love it. I'll work on that tan for you. Did you know Sophie broke up with Doug before he left on tour? She just told me. I'm literally in shock. She must be too. She hasn't even cried over it. She doesn't want to talk about it, but I'll keep trying. I love you, D.

The nightclub was packed again. We stood by the bar for a while until a table opened up. Liam and his friends were in the club, but they were talking to a group of girls and didn't notice us come in. Sophie ordered a margarita. I passed.

Seriously, only ten seconds after we sat down, two guys walked over to talk to us. "Ladies."

I smiled at them. Sophie ignored them.

"Can I get you a drink?" the taller, redheaded one asked me.

"No thanks, I had a little too much last night."

"Where are you girls from?"

"Vancouver."

"In Canada?"

"That's the place," Sophie said in a condescending tone. The guys didn't seem to notice her attitude.

While I talked to them, Sophie looked around the club, bored. I jumped a little when I felt an arm drape over my shoulders. "Hey, fellas," Liam said. The guys raised their glasses up in the air to toast Liam. There was an awkward silence for a second before they left without even saying goodbye. "The men are like sharks around here," Liam said. "Good thing I'm here to protect you."

"I think we can fend for ourselves," Sophie sneered.

He picked up on her tone and backed off. He was immature, but he wasn't dumb. "Just give me a signal if you want me to swoop in and cock-block for you. Tug your ear and I'll be your instant boyfriend warding off all ill-intentioned suitors."

"The proverbial knight in shining armour," I said.

"Your wish is my command." He attempted a medieval bow.

"You're sweet. We'll signal you if we need anything."

He seemed pleased with the compliment and went back to stand with his friends. He leaned his back against the wall and pointed two fingers at his own eyeballs, then swung his fingers to point at us.

"Are you going to lash out at every person who tries to talk to us?" I asked Sophie.

She shrugged. "They all seem so—"

"Not like Doug?"

"I was going to say lame."

"You may need to lower your standards."

"Why? Because I'm a small-town girl who works as a waitress?"

"No." I frowned at her. "What I meant is that Doug is crazy smart, wickedly talented, and ridiculously unique—not to mention sexy—and worships you. You're not going to find another guy even remotely as interesting as him."

"Thanks for making me feel better."

"I'm not trying to make you feel better. I'm trying to make you feel horrible so you realize what you're about to throw away."

"Well, don't." She got up and walked away towards the restrooms. While she was gone, I had to signal Liam to come over and save me from a group of rugby players. He sat down and took the opportunity to chat me up until Sophie came back to the table. "So, Liam, how many times have you been shot down on this trip?" she asked as she pushed him off her stool and sat down.

"Counting you ladies, probably about forty-seven." He smiled.

"And your success rate?"

"Counting the girl this morning," he looked up at the ceiling as if he was counting in his head, "zero."

"Yet. You don't give up."

"It only takes one yes. You can't win the lottery if you don't buy a ticket."

She pointed at the dance floor. "Well, there's a group of sleazy girls over there. Go buy a ticket. Good luck." She smiled at him in a fake way.

He took the hint and winked at me before he left.

"He's just being nice. You can withdraw the claws," I said.

"He wants to get in your pants, Derian."

"Hi, girls." A sloppy drunk leaned on Sophie's shoulder and tried to grope her chest.

"Watch the hands, cowboy." She pushed his arm off her shoulder and he stumbled a little before regaining his balance.

"Dance with me," he slurred.

"You can barely stand."

"Forget the dancing. Let's go to my room."

"No." She pushed his hands off her again.

"You smell pretty."

Sophie stood and said, "Let's go, Deri."

The guy grabbed her arm and held her close. "Don't rush off. The party is just getting started."

"Let go of my arm or I will drop you."

He laughed. I spun around to try to get Liam's attention because when Sophie made a threat like that she meant it. Things were about to get ugly. Unfortunately, Liam was talking to a girl and wasn't looking over at us. I heard the guy whisper to Sophie, "You're so tiny. I could do whatever I wanted and you wouldn't be able to do a thing about it." He smiled, then leaned in to try to kiss her.

She stomped her foot down on the side of his knee and he collapsed to the floor. I was about to get a bouncer when Liam jogged over. The sloppy drunk struggled to stand, not able to put weight on his right leg. His face was furious and he acted as if he wanted to fight Liam. "What's the problem, man?" Liam asked.

"That bitch tried to blow out my knee."

"Why?"

"She's crazy."

"Yeah, I'm crazy because I don't enjoy being groped and slobbered on," Sophie scoffed. "Touch me again and you'll leave here on a stretcher."

Liam stood in a stance that made it seem as if he was prepared to fight, but the expression on his face told a different story. Fortunately, one of the drunk guy's friends noticed that he was causing trouble. He apologized and escorted the guy away.

"Thanks," Sophie said to Liam. "But I can handle myself. And Derian has a boyfriend," she reminded him. "You're wasting your time."

He nodded slowly, reluctant to leave. Sophie's eyebrow lifted in a threatening way, so he turned to me and said, "Just tug your ear if you need me again."

"Okay. Thanks."

Liam walked away and Sophie signalled the waiter to bring her another margarita. It was Luis. "Hello, Miss Sophie."

"*Hola*, Luis."

"Are you having a nice time, Miss?"

"No. The guys here are pigs. We're leaving as soon as I'm finished this." She tipped her head back and chugged half the margarita.

He laughed.

"They have you working double-shifts?" I asked Luis.

"I need the money. I'm saving for university in the States."

"You should come to Canada. It's cheaper."

"It's colder too."

I laughed. "That's true."

"Would you like a drink?"

"No thanks, I mean *gracias*."

"If anyone bothers you, just let Jose over there know. He's my cousin." He pointed to a bouncer, who was standing in the corner.

Sophie thanked Luis before he walked away. Then she looked back at me and saw something over my shoulder that made the smile drop off her face. "Holy shit."

"What?"

Her smile returned slowly. "You are in so much trouble."

I was scared to look behind me. "Why?"

"A complication just showed up. Mmm, a beautiful complication."

Chapter 8

Someone leaned over my shoulder and spoke into my ear, "That's a beautiful necklace you're wearing."

My breath stopped moving in and out and my heart raced as I recognized the smooth, sweet voice.

He continued in a low, sexy tone, "I bought one like it from a shop in Paris once. The shop keeper told me it was one of a kind."

Sophie's eyes widened in amusement as if she were watching a very entertaining play. My face burned as the blood rushed to my head. "Where is the necklace now?" I asked and closed my eyes so I could imagine his face from memory.

"I gave it to an amazing girl, hoping she would maybe fall in love with me one day." His finger ran down the length of my hair. "The only problem was she loved someone else."

Guilt rose into a lump and made my throat uncomfortably tight. "She sounds horrible."

"No. She's one of the sweetest people on the planet. And if she would turn around I would be able to see her face again."

I spun around on the stool and stood to hug him. He was about ten pounds of muscle heavier than the last time I saw him but still felt familiar. Although we had only dated for a short time, we had shared a special connection. A closeness I never forgot, despite the fact that I hadn't seen him since the day I told him we could only be friends. After I released him from the embrace I leaned back and held either side of his jaw to study his perfect face. He was really tanned and his caramel hair was longer than it used to be. His blue eyes were exactly the same, though. He was wearing casual shorts and a plain t-shirt, but even without the designer clothes, he was still model-handsome. He smiled in his trademark charming way, amused by my shock.

"What are you doing here, Mason?"

He shrugged. "Dreaming, apparently. Hi, Sophie."

"Hi." She grinned, as surprised to see him as I was.

Mason sat down on a stool beside me and I wrapped both my hands around his out of habit. His skin wasn't smooth the way it used to be. It was calloused and rough, like Trevor's. He looked at our intertwined hands and his smile faded as if he wished I hadn't done it, so I slid them away. "You've been working with your hands," I said, suddenly not sure how to act around him, given the fact we hadn't even talked in six months.

"I've been helping with a construction project down here."

I was just about to ask him what kind of construction project when a chocolatey-brown-skinned guy with soft-looking curly hair joined us at the table. "Hey, Bill. Who are your new friends?" he asked Mason.

Sophie and I exchanged a confused glance because he called him Bill. Mason shot us a serious look before he jumped in and said, "We haven't actually gotten to the introductions yet." He extended his hand towards Sophie. "I'm Bill."

She frowned, but played along, "Nice to meet you, Bill. I'm Sophie."

He shook my hand. "Derian," I said hesitantly.

"That's a beautiful name." He smiled his shy smile that I had always adored. "This is my buddy, Orrett."

Orrett leaned in towards Sophie and asked, "Would you like to dance?"

She shrugged in a what-the-hell kind of way and held his hand as they made their way out onto the dance floor.

I turned to Mason. "What's up with him calling you Bill?"

He glanced over his shoulder. "I can't talk about it here. I'll explain when we're alone. Just go along with it."

"Okay." I was confused and still dumbfounded that he was in Acapulco. "I can't believe you're actually sitting here in front of me in Mexico. This is so weird. It's wonderful but weird."

"Definitely." He leaned in so close to my neck that his breath tickled my skin. "Wonderful."

Liam stood a few metres away, watching us intently. He shot me a questioning look and waited, probably wanting me to tug at my ear. Obviously I didn't, which made Liam look a little hurt.

"So, things are still good between you and Trevor," Mason said as he sat back.

I nodded and watched the emotions move through his expression. "Yes."

He smiled in a way that wasn't happy. "I've missed you."

"I've missed you, too."

His eyes met mine to check if I said it conversationally or actually meant it. He had left Squamish without saying good-bye right after Trevor and I started dating. I had often wondered what he was up to and how he was doing. I had definitely missed him and it must have shown in my expression because he smiled.

"I tried to call you on the anniversary of your brother's death. The number I had for you wasn't in service, so I called your parents. Did your mom give you the message?"

"No." He looked over at Orrett and Sophie dancing and licked his bottom lip. "She probably thought she was protecting me."

"Protecting you from what? Me?"

His eyebrows angled into a frown as he nodded subtly. "After you broke things off with me I quit working for my dad and took off without telling them where I was going. My mom thought you were the reason I went MIA."

"I wasn't, was I?"

He ran his finger over the tension in his eyebrow and stared at the table. "Technically, yeah. You were the reason I left, but I felt lost way before I met you. Being with you and then losing you made me realize I needed to find the real Mason again. I spent some time in India and South America. Then I came here."

"And you found the real Mason in Mexico?"

"No." He chuckled. "I haven't found him yet. I'm still searching."

I loved how he was always so open and willing to be vulnerable and genuine with me. The way we got each other on that deeper level was part of what made our relationship so meaningful. It was the part I missed the most about being his friend. But if leaving everything in his past was what he needed to do to figure out what made him happy, I was glad he did it. "What exactly have you been doing here that has turned your decadently soft hands rough?"

"Volunteering for a humanitarian group. My dad was glad I was showing interest in something, so he's funding this project for me. We're building schools for small, remote villages. I come into Acapulco every couple of weeks to get supplies and take a few days off here at the resort."

"How much longer are you going to be in Acapulco?"

"We head back to camp tomorrow afternoon." His eyes met mine in a way that felt like our souls were getting reacquainted, then he asked, "Is it all right if we spend time together before I leave?"

"Of course."

The music seemed to get louder as more people packed into the already muggy club. Mason scanned the crowd as if he was looking for a quiet spot for us to hang out. "Why does that blond kid keep staring at us?"

I looked over my shoulder in the direction Mason had nodded. "Oh, that's Liam. He's our neighbour at the hotel. He knows I have a boyfriend, so he's taken it upon himself to protect me from unscrupulous predators like you."

Mason didn't seem to take it as the joke I intended and stood. "Do you want to go for a walk on the beach?"

"Um." It was stifling and crowded and obnoxiously loud, so I nodded to agree. "Let me tell Sophie first. I'll meet you at the door." I manoeuvred over to where Sophie was on the dance floor and shouted in her ear, "He wants to go for a walk on the beach. Are you okay with Orrett?"

"Yeah, he's cool." Her left eyebrow lifted in a pseudo scold. "Make sure your walk on the beach doesn't turn into anything more than a walk on a beach."

"It's Mason. Not a random guy I met at the bar. He knows Trevor and I are still together. We're just two friends catching up," I said, maybe only partly to convince her and partly to remind myself.

"All right. I'll meet you back at the room."

I hugged her, then before I left spun back around quickly. "I almost forgot. Make sure you play along with the Bill thing. He said he'll explain later."

"Sure. Have fun."

I made my way through the crowd to where Mason was waiting. We left the club and walked down the path towards the beach. Small lawn lights lit the way and the sound of the waves surrounded us as if we were immersed in a relaxation CD. The air was still warm and the stars were incredibly bright. When we reached the end of the path, where it turned sandy, I rested my hand on Mason's shoulder to take my shoes off. Something shuffled behind us and I tensed up as I spun to see what it was.

"It's okay," Mason said. "It's just my bodyguard. He'll stay far enough away to give us privacy."

"Bodyguard? Why do you need security?"

Mason stepped close and glanced around before he whispered, "I don't. My dad's just being over-protective because his company is funding all of the school projects. He thinks if someone finds out who I am that—" He checked over his shoulder. "He's just being over-protective. I don't want anyone to treat me any differently because of my dad. That's why I'm going by Bill. Bill Murray. Do you like it?" He chuckled.

I knew he chose it because Bill Murray movies were his favourite, but I didn't think it was cute. "No." I shook my head. "No. Definitely not. You have to go back home. I don't want you to be in danger."

"I'm not in danger. It's just a precaution. We haven't had any problems."

"Mason," I said in a pleading way.

"Bill," he corrected me.

"I won't be able to sleep knowing that something bad might happen to you while you're here. Can't you search for the real Mason in a place where the real Mason's life isn't at risk?"

"I'll be fine as long as you stop calling me Mason." He tucked my hair behind my ears. "I do like hearing you say my name, though. Say it again," he whispered.

Even though he shouldn't have been acting flirty I was desperate to convince him that his project was dangerous. Hoping I could persuade him, I leaned in really close so my lips were almost touching his ear and whispered, "Mason."

He closed his eyes as if he wanted to savour the sound. "Mmm."

"I'll say it again if you promise to go back home."

He laughed. "I like it here."

"What would I have to do to convince you to come home?"

He raised his eyebrows and chuckled.

I had a fairly good idea what he might have been thinking, so I steered him away from that topic. "What if I just blurted out who you are? You'd have to come home then."

"I wouldn't make it home alive if you did that."

"Oh, Mason." I actually felt panicked that he wasn't taking the risk seriously enough. "I mean Bill, I'm not comfortable with what you're doing."

He stretched his arm across my shoulders casually and encouraged me to stroll slowly with him. "It's totally fine. I've been here for four months and nothing has ever happened. Mostly we just spend time with friendly villagers and a bunch of innocent little kids. It's so safe I would take you there. In fact, why don't you and Sophie come with us tomorrow? You can stay with us for a couple of days, get some volunteer experience, and see that it's completely safe."

"Seriously?" I stopped walking and turned to face him. "It's not safe to travel outside the resort area. There are travel warnings for tourists."

"We travel with armed guards. You'll be safer with us than you are at that nightclub."

I squinted over to where I imagined his bodyguard was lingering, but I couldn't see him. Not sure what I thought about the offer to go with him to volunteer for a couple days, I sat down on the sand and gazed up at the stars, thinking. Mason sat down beside me and leaned back to rest on his elbows as he watched the surf crash on the shore in the moonlight.

Eventually his head shifted and I felt his gaze on me. "You're thinking about Trevor, aren't you?"

I sighed and scooped the sand with my hands and then let it sift through my fingers like an hourglass. "If he were sitting on a beach in Mexico with an ex and contemplating an offer to go into a remote place to volunteer with her, I'm pretty sure I wouldn't be that thrilled with the idea."

"Technically, you and I were never more than friends."

I was quiet again as I was reminded of the feelings I'd had for Mason. He was right, our relationship had been platonic physically. But emotionally it had been more than just friends. At least for me.

Mason rolled onto his side to face me, propped up on one elbow. "Don't you trust Trevor?"

My initial reaction was to say of course I do but I hesitated for a fraction of a second, which Mason noticed. I didn't feel like going into all the details of my recent unwarranted jealousy, so I simply said, "I trust him."

"Then if he were on a beach in Mexico with an old friend you wouldn't have anything to worry about. He loves you." He studied my expression almost as if he knew there was something not quite right about how I hesitated. He reached over and gently poked my arm in a teasing way. "Don't you trust yourself?"

Without answering or even looking at him I laid back on the sand and stared up at the stars. "What do you think the chances are that Sophie and I came to Acapulco on a last-minute whim, and you were in town for only one night, then we went to the same club at the same time?"

"You're the psychic. You tell me."

The chances seemed astronomically slim. More than coincidental. "Did you use your connections to arrange it somehow?"

He chuckled. "No. Apparently the universe arranged it."

If that was true, the coincidence obviously meant something. Another test for Trevor and my relationship, maybe. Or a message. I had read in an intuition book once that there was no such things as coincidences, only messages that we either paid attention to or ignored. I was paying attention, but that didn't help at all with figuring out why our paths would cross in Mexico. I wouldn't put it past him to give Sophie's dad the tickets and orchestrate the meeting, but he seemed surprised to see me, too. Maybe running into him was really just random and meant nothing. I didn't know.

He smiled at the fact that I was trying so hard to unsuccessfully calculate the probabilities. "It's not as random as it seems. My dad is a part-owner of the resort and they market almost exclusively to Canadians. It makes sense that you ended up at this particular resort. And there was a one-in-four chance you'd be here on my once-a-month weekend."

His dad owning the resort was just as much of a coincidence. Of all the cities, all the resorts, all the nights, we ended up in the same place at the same time. Universal intervention felt like the most logical explanation or he paid someone off to make it happen. And I didn't know what to think about that. Eventually I turned my head to look at him and said, "I trust myself."

He smiled in a satisfied way and then laced his fingers behind his head to lie flat on the sand. "How do you like school?"

I didn't answer at first because the change in topic was abrupt and I hadn't fully gotten over the weirdness of running into him. What was even weirder was that it didn't actually feel weird to fall right back into the easy comfort of conversation that we had always shared. "It's hectic. I like my courses, but there's a lot of work. I was actually getting really stressed and needed this vacation."

"What are you and Trevor going to do after he graduates?"

"I don't know. We haven't really discussed that far in the future yet. Why?"

"It's not that far in the future. He's got two years left on his forestry degree and will probably be away for most of his third year on field studies. You've got four more years plus at least a couple years' interning ahead of you if you still plan to become an architect. Trevor will be pretty established in a forestry career by the time you're ready to get a job. You might want to work in New York or internationally since, the last time I checked, the best architect jobs weren't in Britannia Beach. Is he willing to live somewhere else?"

"Um, I don't know. We haven't really talked about any of that in detail." I glanced at him and I could feel my eyebrows angling into a deep frown. "I'm sure we will. We'll figure something out."

He didn't say anything—not in the I-don't-have-anything-to-say-about-that way—more in the I-think-it's-odd-that-you-haven't-talked-to-your-boyfriend-about-the-future-but-I-don't-want-to-judge-you way. It was strange. Trevor and I had been dating for six months. We both knew exactly what we wanted school-wise and career-wise, but we hadn't discussed how those goals would work together. I was only eighteen. It hadn't occurred to me that I had to think about things like that yet, but maybe I did.

Maybe sensing that he had thrown me into a silent panic, he changed the topic and asked, "How's your granddad?"

Relieved to talk about something less terrifying than my undeniably uncertain future, I rolled onto my stomach and rested my cheek on my forearm. "Granddad is good. He moved into a fifty-five-plus condo in Squamish after the new owners took over the Inn. At first he didn't know what to do with all the free time, but now he's going on all sorts of golf trips and sightseeing tours with people he's met in the building."

"Do the new owners make the famous apple-cinnamon muffins as well as you did?"

"Of course not. I used a secret ingredient."

He leaned closer and whispered, "What is it?"

"I could tell you, but then I'd have to kill you." I swiped my hand to flick sand on his arm.

"Ha ha. You do realize that's the first threat I've received since I've been here."

I propped myself up on my elbows. "Not the same. I don't understand why you need to take unnecessary risks to find yourself."

"It's not risky. And I won't be here much longer. I'm starting school in the fall."

"Really? Where?"

"Florida. They have a good marine biology program."

I smiled at the memory of when he first told me he was interested in marine biology. Everyone had assumed he liked working for his dad, making a lot of money, but he didn't. I had challenged him to think about what he really liked and what made him happy, which was one of the things he had said he appreciated about me. "I'm really happy for you. Are you happy?"

He smiled and then said the same thing he'd said on our very first date, "I'm happy right now."

"Still saying provocative things, Mr. Cartwright."

He chuckled. "Not everything has changed, I guess."

I moved and sat cross-legged to face him. In a lot of ways it felt as if nothing had changed. Maybe that was how connections like ours worked—life changed, we changed, but our bond was unaltered. I wondered if that would still be the case in ten, or even fifty, years. "I saw twin boys at the airport that reminded me of you and Cody. Maybe I should have taken that as a sign that I was going to run into you."

The mention of his bother shifted his mood and he sat up to stare out at the waves again. "So, you think about me sometimes?"

I dug my toes in the sand and buried my feet as I contemplated how much to admit. Trevor wouldn't have been overly thrilled to know how often Mason did pop into my head, but there was no reason why Mason shouldn't know the truth. "Every time I see a Range Rover, I check to see if the driver is you. When a Town Car pulls up to the curb, I wait to see if it's you who gets out. The sound of a helicopter flying over the city always makes me wonder where you are. So, yeah, I'd say I think about you sometimes."

He smiled and relaxed again. "I've written you a letter every week since I've been here."

"Really?"

"I didn't send any of them, obviously, but you're the only person who I felt like I could talk to."

"Do you still have them?"

"They're back at the camp."

"Why didn't you send them?"

His eyes widened and he shot me a goofy *duh* look. "Because you have a boyfriend."

"That doesn't mean you can't write to me. Do you have a girlfriend?"

"No." He inhaled and hooked his elbows around his knees. "I wanted to take a break from dating for a while to see if it would help me find myself."

"Cold turkey. Impressive. If you keep that up they won't be able to call you Chance anymore."

"I never liked that nickname."

"And now you're Bill."

His eyebrows angled into a frown. "Yeah, apparently I'm no closer to figuring out who Mason is."

He became quiet and seemed lost in thought. I had no idea what time it was, but it was obviously so late that it was early because the sky started to lighten. I wondered if the bodyguard was still there somewhere in the bushes, and if he was, I wondered when he slept. "Maybe we should get back before Sophie starts to worry," I said.

Silently, Mason stood and extended his hand to help me to my feet. He was staying in the building closest to the lobby but he walked me to the other end of the resort to my building. We ran into Sophie and Orrett on the path. "Hey," she said with amusement. "That was a long walk."

"We were just talking," I said in a quiet but threatening tone to make her drop the teasing she was undoubtedly about to launch into.

"We were just talking," she mimicked me in a high-pitched voice as she brushed the sand out of my hair. Fortunately that was the extent of her ribbing. "You guys want to come in for a drink?" she asked the boys.

They exchanged a look that communicated some sort of silent agreement and followed us upstairs.

Chapter 9

In our suite, Sophie cracked open the mini bar and started mixing different types of booze. While Mason was out on the balcony, Orrett said to me, "You must be quite something. Billy never spends time hanging out with women we meet at the bar, and he's had plenty of opportunity."

I almost told him we already knew each other but remembered that he didn't even know Mason's real name. "You must be quite something too. Sophie doesn't find very many people interesting enough to even give the time of day to, let alone invite them in for drinks."

"Well, I am admittedly cool," he said with a grin. "And we have a lot in common."

"Really? Are you a musician?"

"I used to be. I'm a dentist now."

Sophie joined us in the living room with a tray of four glasses and Mason stepped in from outside. I scooted over on the couch to make room for him to sit beside me. The drink Sophie handed me was too strong for me, so I put it back on the table. "How long have you been working on the humanitarian project?" I asked Orrett.

"Almost a month. I'm going home after this project is finished."

"He's married and has a three-year-old son," Sophie added, as if she wanted to make it clear to me that he wasn't going to be her rebound from Doug. It was hard to tell if she was disappointed about that or not. I was relieved he was unavailable since I couldn't imagine her or Doug being with anyone other than each other.

Orrett choked back a sip of Sophie's burning drink concoction and then said, "Even the people who aren't married don't usually stay longer than a month. Billy's a die-hard—four months and counting."

"Four months?" Sophie exclaimed. "That's a long time to be away from home."

Orrett nodded and added, "I have a theory that he won't confirm nor deny. I think maybe some girl back home broke his heart and he's not ready to go back."

Nervous that my expression would let on to the fact that we knew him I made a joke. "Bill seems more like the type who breaks hearts, not the other way around."

Apparently Mason didn't find the topic particularly humorous. He shifted his weight and then shot back his entire drink. There was a long, awkward silence before Sophie fortunately changed the subject to some obscure punk bands that Orrett also knew a lot about.

I glanced at Mason, wondering if what happened between us the summer before really had made him not want to go back home. We'd only technically gone on a few dates and more than six months had passed since. We hadn't left things on bad terms; although it was sort of an abrupt hey-I-choose-Trevor-thanks-for-everything type of closure, it shouldn't have left lasting scars or traumatic memories that he would want to avoid. Definitely not. His four-month stint probably had more to do with steering clear of his dad's pressure to go back to work, or to break free from the person everyone back home assumed he was, or to escape the pain of losing his brother.

Orrett noticed how intently I was studying Mason's expression, so I stopped and focused on what he and Sophie were talking about instead. But I couldn't help feeling sad that Mason still hadn't found what made him happy. Maybe that's how it was for most people. I was lucky that I didn't have to search my whole life to find it. My happiness had been right next to me all along.

When I glanced over at Mason again he was already looking at me with an intensity that made it seem like he knew what I was thinking.

After another round of gasoline-grade drinks Sophie stood and stretched. "I'm going to get some sleep before it's time to get up again."

Orrett stood and pointed at Mason. "Make sure you get some shut-eye too."

"I'm fine."

Orrett shot him a stern parental-type look before he left.

Mason and I moved and sat on lounge chairs out on the balcony. "What was that look about?" I asked.

"Nothing. I haven't been feeling that well lately. He's just bugging me so I won't get overtired. He knows it means more work for him if I have to take a sick day. I'm fine."

"Are you sure? We can hang out in the morning instead."

"I don't want to go to sleep. I want to talk. I miss our talks."

I smiled. "Me too."

The sky turned gold as the sun rose somewhere behind us and Mason said softly, almost as if he didn't mean to say it out loud, "You're even more beautiful than I remembered."

I wrinkled my nose, uncomfortable with the fact that he did say it out loud, and joked, "You've been in the Mexican wilderness too long."

"No." He stared at me for another second and then focused on the view over the railing. "Trevor's a lucky guy."

It was a sweet thing to say, but it felt like maybe the feelings he used to have were surfacing. I didn't want him to get hurt, and I didn't want there to be any confusion about my status, so I said, "Thank you. I'll tell Trevor you said that."

Mason's expression twitched subtly with an emotion that disappeared again before I had a chance to decipher it. Liam and his friends got home next door. They were being loud initially but then settled down as they either went to bed or passed out. When it was quiet again I asked Mason, "What does your dad think about you going into marine biology in the fall?"

"He hasn't really said anything about it. I think he's hoping it's just a phase."

"Is it just a phase? Do you think you'll start working for him again or actually become a marine biologist?"

He shrugged and crossed his ankles on the balcony railing. "I don't know."

Seeing him in casual shorts and plain t-shirt was a stark contrast from the designer tailored suits and European runway clothes I was used to seeing him in. "It might be hard to give up your lavish lifestyle forever."

He frowned a bit. "No. I like it better when I have to work for things. It makes it easier for me to figure out what I really need when everything isn't just handed to me."

I nodded because that did make sense. I shouldn't have assumed how it would feel to give up the perks of his privileged life. "What have you figured out about your needs so far?"

"It's all in the letters I wrote you. I'll send them. Just don't tell Trevor. I don't feel like getting an ass-kicking."

I laughed at first, but the smile faded as I thought about how he must have felt when I had told him about my feelings for Trevor. "I'm sorry if I hurt you by choosing Trevor."

He shrugged. "You made the right choice. I didn't even know who I was. It was for the best. It happened for a reason."

"Do you really believe that?"

He nodded. "Without a doubt."

Relieved that he was okay with how things turned out, I shoved his shoulder lightly to get him to look at me. "I'm glad we ran into each other. Even if it is just for the day."

"Me too."

We talked for another couple of hours. When the sun rose high enough to hit the balcony Mason stood and stretched as he said, "I'm hungry. Do you want to join me for the breakfast buffet?"

"Definitely. Let me grab a quick shower and change my clothes. I'll see if Sophie's up yet."

When I stood, I had a vision. I was running and jumped over the edge of something very high. I fell until I hit water. Then I saw Trevor's face.

Mason had witnessed my visions before, so he knew what it meant when I zoned out momentarily. He stood in front of me holding my elbow. "What did you see?" he asked quietly.

"I'm not sure. I need to contact Trevor."

Chapter 10

It was so annoying to not have Wi-Fi in our hotel room. I sent Trevor a text, but he didn't respond. It was early, so he was probably still asleep. Or if he was awake, he might have been out for a run. Mason left to shower in his room. I woke Sophie and hopped in the shower first because I wanted to have time to go down to the computer stations in the lobby before meeting the guys for breakfast.

As I brushed my hair in front of the bathroom mirror, Sophie squeezed behind me "Why do we have to call him Bill?" She stepped into the shower.

"His dad is financing the school project he's volunteering for and he doesn't want anyone to know he's related."

"Why?" she shouted over the sound of the water.

"Partly because he doesn't want preferential treatment and partly because it might not be safe if the wrong people find out that he's wealthy."

"What, like he'll get kidnapped for ransom or something?"

"I guess. It's common in some parts of Mexico." I applied clear lip gloss and pulled my hair into a ponytail.

"Shit." She towelled off as she made her way back to the bedroom. Then buttoned the fly on her jean shorts and pulled a tank top over her head. "I hope you know boyfriends aren't an obstacle for guys like Mason. He's smooth enough to make you slip up if you're not careful."

I leaned my shoulder against the doorframe, arms crossed. "We were just talking—as friends. I made it clear I'm still with Trevor. And I love Trevor."

"I know. That's why I'm warning you now." She pointed at me in a genuinely cautionary way. "Be careful."

"Mason didn't even try anything. He's a gentleman."

"He's a sex Jedi." She slipped her feet into sandals and slid a stack of gold bangles onto her wrist. "If he uses the Force on you, you might not be able to resist."

"He leaves this afternoon. I can handle it."

She walked over to me and pinched my cheeks. "I hope so."

I rolled my eyes. "A little faith, please. Meet me downstairs. I need to email Trevor."

I had to wait for a computer. A man who was booking golf tee-times, apparently for the entire year, was using one. One of the computers wasn't working. One was being used by a girl who was messaging someone back and forth at impressive speed per message but torturous speed per conversation. I paced around and tapped my fingers on my thigh. I think I annoyed the golf guy enough that he finally got up and left.

I sat down and logged in to compose the email: *Hi Babe. There's no Wi-Fi in the room and it's ridiculously slow in the lobby so I have to use a shared computer. If you need to get a hold of me you should text. I keep having a vision. I think it has something to do with you getting lost on a rescue. I don't know for sure. Please don't go on any rescues until I get back.*

I sent it and then remembered I had other things to tell him. While I was writing the second message, his response to the first one came through:

Hey, I'm not going up to Britannia Beach. I have way too much studying to do. You don't have to worry about me getting lost, unless I get lost between my room and the library. I didn't know about Sophie and Doug breaking up. I called him to see how he's doing. He's messed up. He said she won't return his calls or emails. He thought they were going to get married. He asked me to ask you to tell Sophie that he loves her and wants to talk to her. Are you having fun?

I quickly finished typing the second email:

There's one other thing I want to tell you. Don't freak out, because there's no reason to freak out. We ran into Mason down here. It was a coincidence and he's leaving this afternoon. We talked last night and Sophie and I are going to meet him and his friend for breakfast. It's no big deal. Just thought you should know since I would want you to tell me if you ran into an ex.

I wasn't sure if he was still online, but I waited and bit at my fingernails. Finally, my inbox chirped.

Thanks for telling me. Have fun.

Relieved, I quickly typed: *I love you. Please be safe.*

Always am. Love you too.

I felt better knowing that Trevor wasn't planning on going on rescues. I also felt better knowing that Trevor trusted me with Mason.

Sophie and the guys were already standing together at the main entrance to the dining hall. Seeing Mason from a distance talking to her made it seem like he had never been gone from my life. He smiled at me from across the lobby as I approached them, and although there were a lot of reasons why we could never really be close friends, that's what I wished for.

The buffet was literally overflowing with fruits, pastries, and artisan breads. There were stations for pancakes, waffles, French toast, and any type of egg dish you could imagine. It put my little continental buffet at the Inn to shame. I went back three times to fill up on different things. My favourite was the Eggs Benny and the tropical fruit salad with cooked muesli. I was stuffed.

"Do you ladies have plans for the morning?" Mason asked after we finished eating.

"Not really. We were thinking about going to the spa," Sophie said as she tipped the waiter.

"The spa can wait. Orrett and I are taking you horseback riding."

Orrett shrugged as if he didn't know that was the plan, but was fine with it. Mason pulled my chair out for me and I saw him slip the waiter another tip. As we passed the buffet, I grabbed an apple to take with us. I assumed we would be going to the horseback riding along the beach at the resort until Mason led us to the front of the hotel and hailed a cab. Well, it was actually more like a motorcycle with a passenger carriage on the back than a cab. There were no seatbelts and the driver drove like a maniac, weaving between other vehicles and pedestrians. Even if we'd been in a vehicle that was more stable than a tin can, I still would have been terrified by his driving.

The horseback-riding ranch was outside the city on top of a rolling hill. The dinky cab could barely make it up the road with all of us weighing it down. When the hill got really steep, the cab chugged and we could have walked faster. The ranch house was a huge Spanish-style estate with a landscaped desert garden and an impressive fountain that pooled down over river rocks and streamed across the property. Mason beat Sophie to the cab driver's tip and grinned at her competitively.

"It's beautiful here," I said in awe. "Wait," I said, then leaned in so I could whisper in his ear, "Where is your bodyguard?"

He touched his finger to his lips and whispered, "Shh." His mouth stretched into a smile that was intended to be reassuring as he continued, "He's here. You're not supposed to see him. If you see him it either means he's not doing his job properly or we're in trouble."

I frowned and glanced around nervously.

An English-speaking Mexican in a huge cowboy hat, brown

boots, and Wrangler jeans with a woven leather belt met us in front of the stables. He showed us around, then outfitted us with four gorgeous horses. My horse was auburn brown with a dark-brown mane and tail. She had a little patch of white hair in the shape of a diamond on her forehead. Her name was Tortuga.

He showed us how to saddle the horses and checked to make sure we did it right. Mine was wrong. Apparently, the saddle would have slipped around as we rode and I would have ended up riding under Tortuga's belly. My stirrups were too short too. I stood back to let the guide fix everything. Tortuga lifted her tail and dumped a pile of manure a foot away from me. It hit the cement floor of the stable and splattered up on my leg.

"Nice," I groaned.

"You have to watch yourself behind a horse." The guide chuckled as if he had known it was going to happen.

After we were all saddled up he gave us a mini-lesson on riding. Sophie had ridden when she was young, so she was off and trotting immediately on her horse, named Zhara. Mason was on a tan-coloured horse, named Rey, with a blond mane and tail. I had never been on a horse in my life, and Tortuga obviously knew it because she wouldn't even walk for me. Mason slapped her butt and she reluctantly followed the rest of them.

The trails led up over the rolling hills and entered a forested area. My horse was doing whatever she wanted and I kind of wished I could flutter my eyelashes at her to make her do what I wanted. At one point, even though I was yanking on the reins and shouting at her, she walked off the trail and right into a bush. She just stopped and stood with her head in the branches. I didn't know how to make her back up, so Mason had to grab her bridle and pull her sideways until she turned around and followed the trail.

Eventually, I got a bit more confident and she started to listen to me, sort of. We rode for over an hour to the highest peak, which overlooked Acapulco and the ocean beyond. Mason manoeuvred his horse next to mine and the horses leaned into each other and put pressure on my leg. Tortuga was doing it on purpose to be a pest.

"What do you think?" Mason asked as he gazed out at the view.

"It's amazing. Thank you. Do you come here a lot?"

"No. I heard about it from some of the other volunteers, but I've never had a reason to come before."

He dismounted gracefully. I slid off awkwardly. The guide set a picnic table with nice linens and Mexican dishware. He spread out an assortment of authentic, home-made Mexican food and poured us each a wine glass of Sangria from a cooler. I gave my Sangria to Mason, but ate more than my fair share of breads, bean dips, salsa, and other goodies.

After we finished eating, Sophie said, "This was really cool. Thanks Ma—" She stopped herself before she finished saying his name and a panicked expression flashed across her face. Mason and I pretended not to hear it. Orrett didn't seem to notice.

"My horse already doesn't like me," I said to break the silence. "She's not going to be thrilled when she realizes I just put on ten pounds of Mexican snacks."

"You need to give her a good kick to make sure she knows what you want," Mason said as he helped the guide pack everything back into the picnic basket.

I stood to help wrap up the leftovers. "I don't like hurting her."

Mason sort of scoffed and then shot me a glance that wasn't particularly friendly. "Sometimes being too nice hurts more."

He was definitely talking about us and the past. The guilt made me wince. When he saw the expression on my face, his eyes closed as if he maybe regretted saying it. But he was entitled to be mad. It was fair. I deserved it. "Sorry," I said, under my breath, before I walked over to my horse and attempted to get back on. I hopped three times before I gained enough height to throw my leg over her back. Just when I was almost mounted, she spun around and bucked. I was catapulted forward over her shoulder and flipped once before landing on my back in the dirt.

"Ow," I groaned.

Mason was already kneeling beside me when I opened my eyes. "Don't try to move," he said as he scanned my body for blood or sideways bones.

The guide reined in my horse and Sophie crouched down on the other side of me. "Oh my God. Are you hurt?"

"Um." I closed my eyes and took a physical inventory. "My phone is broken, but I think I'm okay." I moved to pick up my shattered phone and a sharp twinge shot through my arm from the elbow to my fingers. "Ow. Maybe not."

"Orrett's a doctor," Sophie said, and moved so Orrett could look at my wrist.

"I'm a dentist," he corrected her.

She waved him over eagerly to indicate that anyone with medical knowledge would do.

"I guess I can take a look." He moved the joint in a couple of ways and it hurt so bad when he bent it back I started to cry. "It might be broken. You need x-rays. Do you have travel medical insurance?"

"No." I sucked back the pain so I could talk. "We left so quickly. I didn't even think about it."

"It's fine. I'll cover the cost," Mason said. "The hospital is on the way back to the hotel."

With help, I got to my feet, but I hadn't even been a good rider with two hands, so the guide phoned the ranch and arranged to have someone pick me up in a Jeep. Mason insisted on riding with me. Sophie and Orrett rode back with the horses and the guide. The drive over the mountain terrain was actually bumpier in the Jeep than it had been on the horse and my wrist started to swell.

Mason looked so concerned. "I'm sorry."

I glanced sideways at him while cradling my wrist against my chest. "It's not your fault."

He reached over and gently touched the swelling on my wrist. "Come with us to the project. I would feel better if you were with us—to make sure your wrist is healing properly."

I shook my head. "I don't think that's a good idea. It's not safe away from the resort."

"You don't have any medical insurance. It's better if you're around a doctor."

"He's a dentist and I've broken my wrist before. I'll be okay once it has a cast or brace."

"We have an entire medical team there." He leaned closer and shifted into a deep and smooth tone that he undeniably knew was charming, "And I want you to come."

"Thank you for the offer." I closed my eyes before I continued so I wouldn't have to see his face, "But I love Trevor."

"I know that." He chuckled as if that wasn't why he was suggesting it. "Do you have a problem with us being only friends?"

"No." I shook my head, confused by the mixed messages. "I just want to be clear, so nobody gets the wrong impression." I paused and looked directly in his eyes for emphasis. "And so nobody gets hurt."

He smiled as if he thought my concern was misguided and cute. "I just thought you and Sophie would enjoy the humanitarian experience."

"Oh." I felt embarrassed for assuming he wanted to be more than friends with me. But even if he didn't have ulterior motives, going with him to the camp was a bad idea for a lot of other reasons too. "Well, thanks anyway, but I thinks it's best if Sophie and I stay at the resort."

He nodded and didn't say anything else about it.

At the hospital, Mason talked with the people at the front desk. Whatever he said to them, or slipped them, resulted in preferential treatment. There was a waiting room full of people and we didn't even have to wait to see a doctor. The x-rays showed that the bone was slightly fractured. They gave me a brace and we were finished in just over an hour.

As we waited in front of the hospital for a cab to take us back to the resort, I sat down next to Sophie on the curb while the boys went across the street to buy water. Sophie smiled in a way that meant she had a plan. "Mason invited us to go with them to the school project for a couple of days."

"And you told him no, right?"

She tilted her head from side to side to indicate that wasn't exactly the answer she gave.

"Are you crazy? They travel with armed guards because it's too dangerous."

She waved off my concern. "Nothing has ever happened. Orrett's wife came down and stayed with him for a few days and she loved it."

"No. You can go. I don't want to."

"You can't let me go by myself. That would be friendship negligence. It's only for two nights. The bus goes back and forth every third day. Mason said the experience will change our lives. Guaranteed."

"Have you forgotten that you warned me to stay away from the sex Jedi?"

"Don't worry about that. I'll run interference." She clasped her hands together in an overly dramatic pleading gesture. "Please. I've always wanted to volunteer on a humanitarian project."

I rolled my eyes at her manipulation tactics, and not that I was even close to considering it, I asked, "How far away is the camp?"

"About two and a half hours. Mason said he'll ride back down to Acapulco with us if you want."

"I can't do any hard labour with my wrist like this. What kind of work do they do?"

"He said we'll probably be painting or something. But you don't have to do anything if you can't manage with your wrist."

"There are probably snakes there. Are you sure you want to be sleeping out in the wilderness?"

She shivered in disgust. "He didn't mention snakes, but he did say we'd be in a two-person tent that's built up on a wooden platform. It has foam bedrolls."

"And snakes slithering beneath the platform," I reminded her, since she was basically phobic of even harmless garter snakes.

"It will be good for us to step outside our comfort zone." She shoved my shoulder. "Live a little."

I shook my head, not ready to cave in. "The food is probably disgusting compared to what they have at the resort."

Mason and Orrett returned and heard me. Mason chuckled and handed us each a bottle of water. "The mess tent is not as good as resort dining. I'm not going to lie." He winked at me. "But when you take away all the fancy amenities that you take for granted you find out what's really important to you."

Torn, I sighed without taking my eyes off him. I could feel Sophie jigging around in anticipation of my final decision. "Three days, two nights, armed guards?" I asked, still skeptical.

"Perfectly safe. I wouldn't take you if it wasn't. The bus leaves from the resort at four o'clock if you're coming."

The cab arrived and Sophie bounced up all excited. "So?"

She and Mason both looked convinced that I was going to give in and say yes. Even though I was leaning that way I said, "I'll think about it," and then climbed into the cab.

Chapter 11

I told Mason that we'd meet him at the bus at quarter to four, whether it was to say good-bye or to join him I wasn't sure. Sophie sat on the couch as I paced in our room. "Lend me your phone. I need to text Trevor," I said after I remembered that mine was shattered.

"I didn't bring it."

I stopped pacing and faced her. "Why?"

"I didn't want to be tempted to contact Doug."

I sat down next to her, hoping she was ready to talk about their break-up. "Trevor called Doug and apparently he's pretty messed up." I glanced over to gauge her reaction.

She shrugged, unfazed. "He was just surprised because he didn't see it coming. He'll get over it after he's been on the road for a while."

Not buying her tough-as-Teflon act I said, "He asked Trevor to ask me to ask you to call him or respond to one of his emails."

She stood and changed the subject as she headed to the bedroom, "I'm going with Mason. Make up your mind if you're coming with me or not?"

She threw enough clothes for three days into her bag. She knew I wouldn't let her go alone and she obviously knew I was at least considering it and would take the risk if she pushed me. Without saying anything I got up and packed my bag in a rush because I wanted to have time to stop at the computer stations on our way to meet the bus.

Liam and two of his friends arrived back at their room as Sophie and I stepped out into the hall. "Ladies," he said and pretended to tip a non-existent hat. "Whoa. What happened to your arm?"

"I fell off a horse."

He frowned at our bags, confused. "Are you leaving?"

"Just for two nights."

Liam's friends went into their room, but he hesitated. "You're not going with those guys you met at the bar last night, are you?"

"Why?"

"It's not safe to travel outside the resort, especially with guys you don't even know."

"We'll be fine," Sophie said and threw her bag over her shoulder as she walked down the hall towards the elevator.

Liam looked genuinely concerned, so I said, "I actually know the one guy from back home. He's a friend of mine, so you don't need to worry."

"Does your boyfriend know?"

"I'm going to send him an email right now."

He stepped back, obviously not in agreement that it was a good idea but also not in a position to argue with me about it. "All right. I'm not the boss of you. Have fun."

"Thanks. And if I don't see you before you leave, bye."

"Bye." He gave me a wave and then opened the door to their room and disappeared. I ran to catch up with Sophie.

Notices were taped to each of the computer screens in the lobby. The internet wasn't working. "Shit. I'll be right back," I said to her and sprinted back to catch the elevator. I knocked on Liam's door. I could hear their voices, but it took forever for him to answer. "Hi, Liam. Can you do me a huge favour?"

"Maybe. What's in it for me?" He grinned.

"Nothing is in it for you. The internet isn't working right now. I was wondering if you could send this message to this email." I scribbled Trevor's email address and a note on the piece of paper:

Sophie and I are heading out of the resort area for two nights to volunteer at the school project Mason has been working at. I'll email when we get back.
Love Derian.

Liam read the note and stuffed the paper in his pocket. "Okey dokey."

"Don't forget." I pointed at him and shot him a stern expression.

"Being responsible is my forte."

Although that was definitely not true, I said, "Thanks," then rushed back to the elevator and made it to the old blue school bus one minute before four o'clock. Mason was waiting for me on the sidewalk. Sophie was already on board. "Everything okay?" he asked.

"Yeah," I said breathlessly. "The internet is down, so I asked Liam to email Trevor for me."

"That blond kid from the bar?" He chuckled. "I bet you one thousand dollars that he forgets to do it."

"You'd probably win that bet." I tapped his arm to remind him he wasn't supposed to be wealthy. "But where would Bill Murray get a thousand bucks from?"

"Good point." He pushed me by the shoulders to board the bus. "You can call Trevor when we get to camp. We have a satellite phone."

The bus was really old and apparently had no shocks. It stunk a little, too. Or the stench might have been coming from one or two of the motley crew of volunteers. The Mason I knew did not, in any way, fit in with such an earthy and shaggy group of people.

Surprisingly, he seemed completely comfortable with them. Maybe even happy.

He noticed I was staring and smiling at him. "What?"

I leaned in and whispered into his ear. "The you that I knew was too clean-cut to be travelling under these conditions."

He pressed his finger up to his lips and whispered, "Shh." Then he looked around to see if anyone was listening and said, "That wasn't the real me. Remember?"

"And this is?"

He shrugged. "Maybe."

"You smell too good for that to be true."

He laughed.

The bus ride was loud and increasing stuffy. It was fun, though. The scenery, once we got out into the countryside, was really unique compared to anything I'd ever seen before. Donkeys, goats, and chickens just wandered around on the side of the road. I slouched down and wedged my knees up against the seat in front of me to get comfortable. "So, Bill, where are you from?" I winked at him.

"Ottawa."

"Oh." I wasn't sure what I expected he would say, but for some reason it surprised me that he said that instead of Squamish. But, then again, he had only lived there for one year.

"How about you?"

"I'm from a little village called Britannia Beach. In British Columbia. It's between Vancouver and Whistler, near Squamish. You wouldn't have heard of it."

"Actually, I think I have heard of it. Is there an historic Inn there?"

"Yes. I grew up in that Inn. My granddad owned it."

"Hmm." He smiled. "Small world."

"Yes. It is a very small world."

I leaned my head back on the seat and was completely relaxed until I caught a glimpse of the machine gun strapped to the guard who was sitting on the first seat. The other uniformed guard who openly carried a weapon was sitting at the back of the bus. I scanned the people on the bus and wondered which one was Mason's personal bodyguard. None of them looked particularly burly. If I had a bodyguard I would want him to look like Murphy.

Sophie and Orrett talked the entire time. I eavesdropped a little. He was telling her about the band he used to play in when he was in high school and university. They liked all the same music and he had even toured as a roadie with some band she idolized. He told her she should keep working on the music, but not discount going to university. It was as if her dad had paid him to say all the right things. I also heard her mention that she'd been toying with the idea of becoming a teacher. I didn't even know that. I thought she told me everything, but I had no clue about that, or Doug. Maybe she would have told me if I hadn't been so preoccupied with school. Knowing that I had been neglecting our relationship made me worry again about the consequences of neglecting my relationship with Trevor.

"What are you thinking about?" Mason asked.

"The many ways I could be a better friend."

He didn't respond at first, and he seemed surprised. "I've never met anyone who is a better friend than you."

"Thank you, but lately I've been a little too focused on myself." When I looked at him, I noticed the dark circles under his eyes. "Are you feeling okay?"

He nodded. "Just a little tired."

"You should try to sleep."

He shook his head. "I'm okay. I'd rather hear more about you."

"Well, I refuse to speak until after you've had a nap. It's my first act of kindness on the path to becoming a more attentive friend."

"Fine." He smiled and took my sweatshirt to prop it against the window. "I'll have a five-minute nap. That's it."

He slept for over an hour, but when we pulled off the main road and headed down a winding dirt trail, the off-roading bounced him awake. "Hey, sleepy head."

Still groggy, he stretched and rotated his head to unkink his neck. It was weird to think that just a few days earlier I had been sitting in a classroom in rainy Vancouver listening to a lecture on modern design. From that to a five-star luxury resort to a remote part of the Guerrero State that definitely didn't get many tourists. Mason's life was so different from mine.

"I can't believe I'm here," I said.

"I can't believe you're here either." His tone was hard to read. He smiled as if he was happy that I decided to come along, but there was something more serious in his eyes that made it seem like maybe he knew deep down that spending time together would inevitably just make the good-bye harder.

When we eventually arrived at the camp, a bunch of little kids ran to meet the bus. As the volunteers filed out, they handed the children things like pencils and erasers and colouring books. Mason gave Sophie and me a Raggedy Ann-like doll each so we wouldn't be empty-handed. I offered my doll to the most precious-looking girl. She was probably about four years old, with bare feet, and big brown eyes. She hugged the doll and then hugged me around my legs. I was instantly in love.

Mason showed us our tent first so we could put our bags down. Then he gave us a tour of the construction site. The school was pretty much built. Most of the work that was left to do was on the inside. They had volunteers who were plumbers, electricians, and dry-wallers, plus they used local tradesmen to do the carpentry. Mason's job was to organize the volunteers and step in to any job where they were short-handed. Orrett was doing dentistry for the villagers and he helped with the construction only if someone got sick or hurt. The rest of the medical team consisted of a nurse, an optometrist, and a surgeon. Mason's dad obviously spared no expense and their equipment looked state-of-the-art. I wondered if they only travelled in a beat-up bus to appear less wealthy while they were on the road.

It started to get dark quickly because of where we were located nestled in the mountains. Since there were no street lights and it was cloudy, it got pitch-dark. I didn't like it. I held one of Mason's hands and one of Sophie's hands wherever we went. Mason carried a lantern and never went more than a foot away from me. He showed us to the mess tent for dinner. The food wasn't quite as bad as I imagined, but it wasn't exactly good.

"You've been eating this for four months? You should talk to the guy who's funding this project and get the menu upgraded," I joked.

Sophie laughed. Mason gave me the same stern look that my grade-two teacher used to scare me with. Then he smiled. "I apologize if it's not up to your five-star-hotel standards, Miss Derian and Miss Sophie."

"Are you calling us snobs?"

"Yes. I bet you're accustomed to flying around in helicopters or private jets and driving around in chauffeur-driven Town Cars or expensive Italian sports cars."

I shot him the stern-teacher look and said, "Mr. Murray, you shouldn't judge me. You don't even know me."

"I know your type." He pointed his fork at both of us and winked. "You're all the same."

I raised my eyebrow to accept his challenge to banter. "You're wrong."

Orrett joined us at the table with a tray and seemed amused by the animated discussion. "Fighting already? You just got here."

"We're not fighting." Mason shrugged and chuckled. "Derian slagged the conditions here. I'm not sure she's cut out for roughing it in the wilderness."

"You're judging me without even knowing me," I said and shovelled some off-white slop into my mouth.

"All right, then, I'll give you one chance to prove yourself."

"Only one chance?" I almost gagged and struggled to swallow whatever it was that I just put in my mouth. After a sip of water to wash everything down I said, "Even I would be willing to give a person more than one chance to prove themselves."

Mason's eyes met mine and he grinned because he knew I was referring to the first time we ever went out. "All right, I'll give you the benefit of the doubt if you eat all your dinner."

My fork hung hesitantly over the plate, not sure I could choke all of it down. Sophie, Orrett, and Mason all scooped up the blah food as if they thought it tasted good. Maybe I was a snob.

"How's the wrist feeling, Derian?" Orrett asked between forkfuls.

"It's throbbing a little."

"I'll give you some Tylenol 3s before you go to bed. They should knock you out."

"Thanks." I ate a few more bites, alternating between sips of water, because Mason was watching me with a satisfied look on his face. I finished the slop and kept the bread for last because I assumed it would be the best-tasting part. Fortunately it was. "What time do we get up in the morning?"

"Six," Mason said and collected our trays to return them.

"He's joking, right?" Sophie asked Orrett in a panic.

"Nope. We wake up at six, eat breakfast, and start working. It's cooler in the morning."

Sophie groaned. "I have to go to bed now then. Where did Ma—" she stopped herself from saying his name, glanced at me, and started over with a completely different question. "I'm really not a morning person. Do you think I can get some of those Tylenol 3s too?"

Orrett laughed because she was genuinely worried about the early wake-up call for hard labour.

"I'm serious. If you guys don't want your faces ripped off in the morning, I need to go to bed now," she said and looked around the room. "Where's Bill? I'm not walking around in the dark by myself."

Mason came back and walked us to the bathrooms, which looked like a classroom portable. He waited outside, and when we were done he walked us to the medical tent for the painkillers and then back to our tent. Sophie unzipped the flap and crawled in. I stood outside with Mason to say good night. He turned off the lantern and I couldn't see his face. He stepped closer and his fingers slid down my arm to my hand as if he wanted to hold it. I might have been wrong. It was dark. Maybe it was an accidental touch. Regardless, I moved my arm to make his hand fall away from mine.

He leaned in and whispered in my ear, "I'm really glad you're here."

I closed my eyes for a second before I responded, "I'm glad I'm here, too. Thanks for the horseback riding, and the broken arm, and the medical treatment. Oh, and thanks for the average dinner. I'm not a snob."

"I know." He laughed. "Good night, Derian."

"Good night, Bill."

"It's just the two of us. You can call me Mason."

"Good night, Mason."

I didn't see him leave. I could only hear his footsteps getting quieter as he got farther away. I climbed into the tent and flopped onto the bed. Sophie rolled over and muttered, "He's working you. Be careful."

I didn't say anything because it felt like maybe she was right.

Chapter 12

The next morning I woke up to the sound of tapping on our tent frame. Sophie groaned and pulled the sleeping bag over her head. I sat up and crawled over to unzip the door. Mason had a big grin on his face. "Rise and shine. Breakfast is in ten minutes."

I rubbed my eyes.

"You look cute in the morning." He winked.

Not sure if he was teasing or flirting, and uncomfortable with both, I patted my frizzed hair down. "We'll meet you at the mess tent."

After a slight pause, where it felt like he was trying to interpret my tone, he nodded before he turned and walked away. I watched him for a while, then crawled back inside to try to wake Sophie up. I got dressed and poked her one more time. She threw a shoe at me as I crawled out of the tent, which was relatively civil for her that early in the morning. I knew she wouldn't get up for breakfast, but she'd be ready to work.

In the mess tent, I sat down at the table with Mason, Orrett, and the nurse. I looked down at the tray of food in front of me and tried to figure out what the yellowy goop was exactly. "Is this eggs or oatmeal?"

Mason chuckled. "Just eat it. You're going to need the fuel because I'm going to work you like a donkey today."

"I have a disability." I held up my brace. "Because of you, I might add."

"All I did was take you horseback riding. You're the one who tried to mount a temperamental horse from the wrong side."

"Fine, my disability might be due to my own inexperience. It still hurts, though."

"All right, you can be my assistant."

"What does your assistant have to do?" I asked warily.

"Whatever I tell her to do."

I rolled my eyes and wrinkled my nose. "I'd rather haul lumber or dig an irrigation ditch."

"I can arrange that." He made a face back at me and reached over to tickle my waist.

Okay. That one was definitely a flirty thing. Orrett and the nurse exchanged glances with each other, as if they were amused with our bantering. "You two act like you've known each other forever," the nurse commented.

"Thank goodness we haven't," Mason said without missing a beat. "I don't think I could tolerate large doses of her."

"Are ya sure?" Orrett asked in a goading way. "I haven't seen you smile this much in the entire time I've been here."

My face felt as if it burst into scarlet blotches. Mason's face didn't blush, but he ran his finger along the scar that cut through his eyebrow. "I smile," he defended himself.

"Not like that," the nurse agreed and stood up with her tray. "Have a good day, everyone." She stopped and turned to say one more thing to Mason, "I sent your lab work in. I should have the results soon."

Mason pressed his lips together in a polite I-wish-you-hadn't-said-that kind of smile, but said, "Thanks."

Orrett patted Mason on the back and stood up with his

tray. "It's good to see you looking happy, man." He pointed at me and added, "Don't let him work you too hard."

He walked away and left Mason and me sitting at the table in silence. I tasted the yellowy goop. It wasn't too bad—whatever it was. Mason watched me as he twirled a spoon between his fingers.

"What lab work?" I asked.

"They made me do some blood tests because I haven't been feeling that well. Just routine. No big deal."

"What do they think it is?"

"It's most likely a low-grade virus or possibly a parasite." He leaned his elbows on the table in an avoidance tactic that I didn't fall for.

"Both Orrett and the nurse seem worried."

He shook his head to dismiss the concern. "You're the one who should be worried." With a mischievous grin he took the spoon from my hand and licked both sides before giving it back. "It might be a rare contagious jungle fever and I just contaminated you."

"Stop pretending it's not serious."

"It's not." He sat back and his mood shifted. "I'll take some medication and be fine."

"And what about earlier? They both said they haven't seen you this happy." I made eye contact with him to make sure he knew I wasn't going to let him brush everything off with a joke. "If it's because I'm here, we need to talk about that. I came here because I thought we could be friends. If that's not how you feel and you're hoping for something more, I should go back."

He uncrossed his arms and sat forward again "I don't want you to go."

"Well, I don't want to be here if you're hoping to be more than friends. I'm sorry if I wasn't clear about that."

"You were clear. You love Trevor. I respect that." He stood with his tray. "I just want to enjoy the time we do have together—as friends."

I felt bad for pushing the point when he hadn't stepped over the line. I just wanted to remind him there was a line. "I don't want you to get hurt when I leave."

"I'm a big boy." He reached over to stack my tray on his. "Stop stalling. You're not going to get out of working."

I didn't want to make a big deal about it if it didn't need to be, so I stood and followed him. Without saying a word to each other, we walked to get Sophie from the tent. I brought her a cup of coffee and, as I suspected, she was at least dressed for work. She was still curled up on the cot, though, so Mason went in and lifted her up, draped her over his shoulder like a fire fighter, then ran and made a motion like he was going to throw her in the creek.

"Do it and I'll say the M word," she threatened.

He immediately put her down and raised his hands in the air to surrender.

She pointed at him with a cautionary glare. "Don't mess with me."

He laughed. "Right, I almost forgot how ferocious you can be."

"Some things never change," she said sweetly.

"No." He glanced sideways at me. "Some things don't. Come with me. You two are on special assignment today."

We followed him towards the construction site. His comment stuck with me as we walked. Hopefully his feelings weren't the 'some things' that didn't change. Even if that was what he meant, we were only staying one more night. How much emotional damage could be done in forty-eight hours?

We passed a group of volunteers getting buckets of paint ready. I liked painting and it wouldn't be too bad with just one hand. But Mason kept walking towards some people arranging trees for planting. I liked gardening too, but my cast would probably be a bit of a pain. He kept walking, right past the construction site. Into the forest. "Uh, where are we going?" I asked, not comfortable being away from the camp.

"You'll see. It's a surprise." He turned and grinned at me when he said it because it's what he used to always say to me. Surprises were his thing.

As we got further away from the volunteers, I heard children playing beyond the trees. After another minute of hiking along a narrow path we arrived in a grassy clearing that was full of children in school uniforms. The boys wore navy-blue shorts and white polo shirts. Most of them were chasing a soccer ball around, a few sat in the shade under a tree. The girls wore navy-blue jumpers over white blouses. Most of them were busy skipping rope and doing cartwheels, a few were playing catch.

The three-sided, slanted-roof building on the far side of the clearing looked kind of like a picnic shelter but served as the existing school. A woman, who I assumed was the teacher, set lesson books out on the three rows of benches. As we crossed the field, she saw us and waved. "*Hola, Señor* Murray."

The children heard her and came rushing to swarm around Mason. They gave him high-fives and hugs. He said something in Spanish that made them all stand perfectly quiet with their hands pressed against their sides. He surveyed each child, then smiled at one boy, who was standing particularly still. It appeared he was holding his breath and trying not to blink. Mason pulled a shiny metal toy car out of his shorts pocket and gave it to the boy. The other kids seemed so happy for him for earning it and they patted him on the back.

Mason looked at us and winked. "Come on, I'll introduce you to Gabriela. She's the teacher. You're going to be helping her today. Are you both okay with that?"

"Absolutely," Sophie said with a level of enthusiasm that I hadn't heard her use about anything in a long time.

Mason and I both watched as Sophie jumped right in to play soccer with the boys.

Orrett must have told Mason that Sophie was considering going into education. He had always been so thoughtful and that definitely hadn't changed. It was the perfect opportunity for her. "Thank you," I said as I turned to face him. "Still in the business of making people's dreams come true, I see."

His face was already lit up from seeing how happy he had made Sophie, but his smile widened even more. "Like I said, some things don't change."

"Apparently."

He introduced me to Gabriela and once we were settled, Mason left to go back to the construction site. Gabriela was so sweet. Her English was not great and since Sophie took Japanese in high school and I took French, our Spanish was too horrendous to communicate well with her. We got by with hand gestures and the little boy who earned the toy car from Mason translated what he could for us. His name was Hector and he spoke English quite well. The language the children were speaking to each other was their native language. According to Hector, only about half the villagers spoke Spanish and very few spoke English.

"How did you learn English?" I asked Hector.

"*Señor* Murray. He teaches me. He teaches all of us. I learn the best."

"You do learn the best," I said.

The children did a writing lesson first. Sophie and I handed out books when asked and collected papers when the children were finished. Gabriela also recruited us to say the English vocabulary words on their spelling test. Midway through the morning, the students got a break, like a recess. I played soccer with one group of students and Sophie sang songs to a group under a tree. The children adored her singing and she ended up having quite a large crowd of kids around her. Gabriela noticed and brought a guitar out of a storage shed for Sophie to play. Eventually, all of the children joined the circle on the ground near Sophie. She taught them silly songs that we had learned at summer camp when we were kids. The kids laughed when I did the accompanying actions for "The Wheels on the Bus", even though most of them didn't have a clue what we were singing about. Gabriela also played a few Spanish songs that the children sang along to.

After the break, the children did a math lesson, which I could actually help them with since it was just addition for the younger children and long division for the older children. The last lesson before lunch was a craft, so we helped with that too. Well, I did what I could with one good hand and the fingers of my braced hand. Hector worked really hard and tied more pieces of ceramic and glass to his wind chime than everyone else. His was so adorned that it was almost too heavy for the string that he used at the top.

"Miss Darianna," he said to me. "Please. Give to *Señor* Murray. Much thank you." He handed me his heavy wind chime.

"He's going to love it. You can give it to him yourself, though. He's right over there." I pointed over Hector's shoulder at Mason, who had just stepped out of the forest and was walking towards us across the clearing.

Hector ran towards Mason, a bit lopsided because the wind chime was weighing him down on one side. Mason picked him up and gave him a hug. They talked for a while in Spanish, then Hector ran off. Mason continued over to Sophie and me. "So, how'd it go?" he asked.

"I loved it," I said. "But are we done already? It's only lunch."

"They only have classes in the mornings. You can help out again tomorrow if you want to."

"I would love to do that," Sophie said, still beaming from the experience. "The kids are absolutely adorable. I'm so glad we came here. I can see why you've stayed for so long."

"Yeah." He nodded and glanced around. "It's rewarding."

"What's next?" she asked.

"Siesta. Everyone rests while it's hot. First we eat a big lunch, then you can go back to your tent and take a nap."

"Sanctioned naps. I officially love this place," Sophie chirped and headed across the clearing.

I turned to face Mason. "Thanks for setting this up. Sophie has been going through some stuff and I think this is just what she needed." I hugged him, partly out of a genuine desire to do it and partly out of habit, but it felt strange. I ended it abruptly and rushed to follow Sophie, so it wouldn't seem as awkward.

Mason caught up to us before we entered the forest and I could tell without even looking at him that he was smiling. When we got back to the construction site, Mason hung his gift from Hector outside his tent and then we all headed to the mess tent together. He wasn't kidding when he said they ate a huge meal. It was actually good too, or maybe I was just really hungry.

After lunch, Mason walked us back to the tent and Sophie crawled in. I was about to kneel in behind her when he grasped my elbow and then pressed his finger to his lips. "Shh." He smiled and motioned with his finger for me to join him. "I want to show you something."

I bit at my bottom lip as I studied his expression. "What is it?"

"A surprise." He extended his arm and wrapped his hand around mine.

I glanced down at our intertwined fingers.

"Trust me." He tugged gently. I did trust him and I was curious, so I followed him down a path on the other side of the village. It led through dense trees that reminded me of the forest in Britannia Beach. We reached a field of big boulders and climbed over them one at a time. Eventually, we reached a secluded pool of water that was shaded by the trees. It was fed by a small waterfall and trickled into a stream below. The trees formed a canopy to block just enough of the sun to make it the perfect temperature.

"Remind you of anything?" he asked as he sat down on the soft, bright-green carpet of moss and grass mixed together.

I nodded and spun slowly to take it all in. The perimeter of the clearing was thick with waxy green bushes covered in huge blooms of pink tropical flowers. "It's like where we went for our third date."

He smiled, obviously glad that I remembered. I sat next to him and we took our shoes off to dip our feet in the pristinely clear water.

"Do you always come here for your siesta?"

"Sometimes. When I want to be alone."

"Are we alone?"

He raised his eyebrows in a suggestive way. "Why?"

"I'm just a little scared being this far away from the village. Does your bodyguard know where we are?"

"We're not alone—alone enough for privacy, though, if you have something else in mind."

"I have a boyfriend, Bill."

He chuckled. "I know that. You're the one who was insinuating."

I shoved his shoulder lightly. "I wasn't insinuating anything. I was just concerned for my safety."

He lifted his feet out of the water and leaned back on the grass, then pulled my elbow so I would lie next to him. "You can call me Mason when we're alone. And you're safe."

I glanced at him, cautious and reluctant to send the wrong message by having a nap with him. Who naps in the Mexican wilderness? His eyes were already closed. It was a peaceful place. And I absolutely wasn't going to try to find my own way back to the tent. As a silent gesture to firmly establish the friend boundary, I scooted over so there was a body-width between us.

Mason chuckled. "Trevor is really lucky. I hope he appreciates how lucky he is."

"He does."

"Then what are you worried about?"

"Relationships are hard. It's not like you just say I love you and everything is perfect all the time. Trevor and I have to work to keep things going well. Responsibilities get in the way. People get in the way. This," I motioned with my finger between us, "is not helping."

"This is a siesta, outdoors, with a bodyguard lurking not far away." He rolled onto his side and propped himself up on his elbow. "I would never do anything to disrespect your relationship with Trevor. One thing I have figured out about myself is that I value integrity."

My head turned to check his expression. It was genuine, as usual. And even though I already knew that on some level it did make me feel more comfortable to hear him say it.

"It's just a nap, Derian. Okay?"

I nodded and rolled to lie on my side. The sun filtered through the leaves and warmed my skin in little patches. The forest was alive with songbirds and it sounded like a relaxation soundtrack that my mom listened to while she soaked in the bath.

I listened to his breathing for a long time before I whispered, "I'm really proud of you. I think you're doing wonderful things here."

Without opening his eyes he said, "Shh. Sleep."

Eventually, I drifted off.

My first couple of dreams were of the kids playing at the school and of Mason showing me surprises. He and I walked up to the Eiffel Tower in Paris and Trevor stood with his back up against the iron base watching us. He didn't look mad; he looked as if he was waiting patiently. Then Mason and I walked along the Great Wall of China. Trevor sat on the Wall watching us. He had the same patient look on his face. Then Mason and I rode on a camel with the Pyramids in the background. Trevor wasn't there. My dream switched to a nightmare as I looked for Trevor. I searched through the sandy desert, then the scenery changed to a forest and I got scared as it turned to night. It was dark and I felt like I was being chased. My heart beat terrifyingly fast. I kept falling down as I ran, trying to reach Trevor. All of a sudden, the earth disappeared beneath my feet and I was falling over the edge of a cliff. I fell and fell before landing in water.

The impact woke me from the nightmare. I sat up abruptly, as if I had been shocked, and accidentally woke Mason.

"What's wrong?"

"I had a bad dream, but it felt like a vision" I stammered between gasps. I stood, trying to catch my breath. I was sweating and shaking. "Something's wrong. I have to call Trevor. I need to use that satellite phone you mentioned."

"It's back at camp." Mason scrambled to his feet and escorted me back.

He disappeared into the administration tent and came out with the phone. I called Trevor's number but it didn't go through, so I tried his dad's number. I figured that if I told Jim I'd had a vision of Trevor getting in trouble on a rescue he wouldn't let him go on one. That call didn't go through either. I tried my mom's number—nothing.

"It's not working." I shoved the phone into Mason's hands as frustrated tears dripped over my eyelashes. "This is a useless piece of junk."

Mason's expression creased with concern. "It will work. But there are only a certain number of voice lines. Sometimes we have to wait for a while."

I paced, wondering if my overly hysterical reaction was due to a legitimate fear triggered by a credible vision embedded in a dream, or if it was some sort of crisis of conscience triggered by guilt. Integrity. Mason had it. Trevor had it. Did I? The visions started before I even ran into Mason, so the siesta dream probably wasn't entirely fueled by my own guilt for disappearing into the forest with Mason without at least telling Trevor first. Bottom line: something was wrong, maybe with Trevor or maybe with me.

"Here. Try again." Mason handed the phone back to me.

I dialled Trevor's number again and, to my relief, it rang through.

"Hello." It was fuzzy, but I could definitely tell it was his voice.

"Trevor, I had another vision. Promise me you're not going on any rescues."

"Deri? The reception is so bad, I can barely hear you. Where are you? I got a cryptic email from a guy who said you took off into the jungle with some random guy you picked up at a bar. What the hell's going on?"

"Sophie and I went with…" The connection dropped before I could tell him where we were. I dialled again without any luck. "Shit." I ran my hand through my hair and paced again.

"We'll try again later," Mason said. "The reception is better at night when it's not as busy."

I shook my head and my jaw clenched.

"We'll get a hold of him. Don't worry. What can I do to make you feel better right now?"

I shrugged. "I don't know." I sighed and handed the phone back to him. "At least I know he's fine. I'll try to call again later."

"What was your nightmare about?"

"I don't know exactly. It was like the visions I've been having where Trevor is missing or lost."

Mason nodded. He'd been with me when Kailyn had gone missing, so he knew there was probably something to take seriously about the visions and the nightmare. He also knew, like I did, that there wasn't much more that could be done unless I saw something specific. "Maybe we should take it easy this afternoon," he suggested. "Something else might come to you if we go for a walk."

"Don't you have to get back to work?"

"They'll be fine without me. Actually, I have something I want to show you. You'll like it. It's a great surprise."

Not sure if I was up for another one of his surprises, my eyes narrowed as I studied his expression. "What is it?"

He grinned like a little boy. "Go get Sophie. She'll like it too."

Chapter 13

I found Sophie in the shade on a picnic table with Hector and two little girls. The younger girl was the one I had given the doll to when we first arrived. She was trying to catch a butterfly in her hands. The older girl, who was probably about eight years old, stood behind Sophie, weaving two braids into her hair. And Hector read out loud from an English story book.

"*Hola*," I said.

"*Hola*, Miss Darianna," Hector replied with a smile that lit up his face. "Miss Sophie is helping my reading to my sisters."

I smiled at the girls. "Your reading is very good, Hector."

"*Gracias,* Miss" He closed his book and said something to his sisters in their native language. "We go. See you later, alligators."

"See you later, alligators," Sophie and I said in unison.

"They are so precious. Maybe I should stay down here," Sophie said.

"Really?" I moved to sit next to her on the picnic table top. "For how long? I would go crazy without you if you stayed for four months."

"You could visit." She shoved my shoulder. "I'm sure Bill wouldn't mind that."

I rolled my eyes. "Trevor would."

"True. Where did you guys disappear to?"

I sighed and picked at the wood of the picnic table. "He took me to a private siesta spot in the forest."

"Derian."

"What? He's being a complete gentleman—we're just friends, like always. Nothing happened."

"But you wanted it to?"

"No." I paused and stared over in the direction of his tent. "I had a nightmare that was like the visions I've been having, where Trevor is missing or lost or something. I called him on the satellite phone and I know he's not planning to go out on any rescues. What do you think it means?"

She studied my expression and then stretched her arm across my shoulders. "I think it means you need to not go on private siestas with Mason."

"I told him we'd go for a hike with him this afternoon. We're supposed to meet him at the mess tent in five minutes."

She shook her head. "Sophie don't hike."

"You have to. He said he has a surprise to show us."

Her eyes rolled dramatically. "I don't have runners."

"You can wear my canvas slip-ons."

Her lip turned up in a pseudo-disgusted expression. "The one's with little hearts and a girly bow on the toe?"

"Yeah, they're adorable."

"Sophie don't do adorable either. You owe me so big."

I jumped up off the picnic table. "Deal."

"Don't think I'm not going to cash in on that promise at some critical moment in our relationship."

"Yeah, yeah. Let's go."

Mason and Orrett were both waiting for us when we arrived at the mess tent. The four of us walked to the dirt road we had driven in on and followed it farther up towards a rugged mountain. We turned off onto a path that I would have never known was there. Sophie wasn't impressed with the physical exertion. I wasn't impressed with being so far from the village. I kept looking behind us to see if I could spot Mason's bodyguard. We hiked for almost an hour without any sign of him.

"It's safe," Mason reassured me when he noticed me looking over my shoulder every two minutes.

"How much farther?" Sophie whined.

"We're here." Mason swung his arm out like a game-show host.

We were in front of a jagged rock face overgrown with vines. "We're where?" I asked.

Mason and Orrett both disappeared behind the edge of the rock. I couldn't even hear their footsteps.

"Where'd they go?" Sophie whispered.

I glanced behind us, partly hoping to see the bodyguard and partly hoping to see no one. "Those idiots better not take off on us. I'll kill him if they leave us here."

"Why would they do that?"

I peeked around the rock. There was a small opening where two edges met. The guys would have had to squeeze through it if that's where they went. I investigated the rest of the crevice without finding any other openings. The cold, black crack in the rock seemed like the only exit route possible.

"I'm not going in there," Sophie scoffed.

"What is it, a cave or something?"

"I don't know and I don't plan to find out."

As we stood there staring at the tiny opening, Mason squeezed back out. "Come on. Are you chicken?"

"Not chicken, just sane," Sophie said.

"Trust me." He smiled his charming smile before he disappeared into the crack again.

"I'm more scared of staying here by ourselves than following him," I said and turned sideways to squish between the rocks.

"Jesus Christ," Sophie huffed and followed me. "If I die in here I'm going to kick all your asses."

"You'll be dead," I reminded her.

"I'll haunt you."

"I'll probably be dead too."

"Great," she muttered.

Once I shimmied through the narrow opening, the space opened up into a huge cavern. It wasn't that dark inside because there were four twenty-foot arched openings along the far side that let light in. Mason and Orrett stood near the edge of one of the openings.

"What is this place?" I shouted.

"An ancient ruin," Orrett hollered back.

Sophie and I walked towards them. As we got closer to the archways, the light revealed that the walls of the cave had primitive carvings on them. I ran my finger over one of the pictures. It was a strange feeling, like being connected to something sacred.

"Wow," Sophie said. "This is amazing."

The view overlooked ruins of a village perched on the mountainside. The piles of stone were crumbling and overgrown with vines, but it was clear that they used to be buildings.

"I've studied things like this in school," I said to Mason.

He made another sweeping hand gesture. "Ancient architecture is best studied in person."

"I see that. Thank you so much."

He smiled and led the way to climb over the edge of the cave and down the mountain towards the ruins. He walked with me as I explored all of the walls and got a feel for how the buildings and the village would have been laid out. It was incredibly interesting, especially since it was completely in its original state. Sophie and Orrett wandered around for a while, but got bored before I was done, so sat on some stone steps talking.

"This would have likely been the temple," I said to Mason excitedly. "Can you imagine what it would have been like to live here then? It's probably almost a thousand years old."

He nodded as he listened to me ramble on.

"These were probably tombs, and look, I think this was for

irrigation. I love it here. Look how short the doorways were. The people must have been tiny. Check this out." I ran my hands over the stonework. "Do you have any idea how difficult it would have been to build this the way they did? It's an architectural marvel."

I scrambled around over the ruins and eventually came across a maze of some sort. Mason followed me as we twisted and turned along the paths, but I made a wrong turn somewhere and we ended up at a dead end. The late-afternoon sun angled down on us and I spotted a stone carving in the wall. I brushed away the dirt and vines to expose a jaguar head.

"Wow. This is so cool." I beamed. "In some myths, the jaguar is said to have the foreknowledge of things to come."

"Like you."

"Yeah." When I turned to face him, he was standing too close. Like chest-to-chest close. Like kissing close.

His gaze met mine, but his expression didn't give any hint to what he was thinking. He didn't step back. He didn't make a move forward, either. For a long, awkward moment.

"Mason," I said quietly, almost as a question.

With his eyes still locked on mine he said in his sexy, charming voice, "I love it when you say my name."

"Don't," I said.

The corner of his mouth turned up. "Don't what?"

Without answering, I ducked past him and rushed down the first corridor.

"Deri," he called after me.

Without looking back I walked faster, winding my way out of the maze. Eventually, I emerged into the village ruins.

Mason caught me by the arm and slowed me down. "I'm sorry."

I shook my head to pretend it was no big deal. "It's fine." I tucked my hair behind my ears and stared down at my shoes to avoid eye contact. "We should get back to the camp while it's still light."

Before Mason had a chance to respond, Sophie screamed in the distance, repeatedly and hysterically.

Mason let go of my arm and we both sprinted to where the screaming was coming from. As soon as I saw Orrett holding a tree branch and her flailing around, I knew exactly why she was screaming and slowed down. Mason didn't, so he ran over to them, panicked.

"There was a huge snake," Orrett explained to Mason.

I laughed because Sophie was dancing around and rubbing her skin violently, as if it was on her or something. Once he knew what the problem was, Mason relaxed and helped Sophie down from the stone wall where she'd perched herself. Movement caught my attention out of the corner of my eye near the opening of the cave. A dark-haired man dressed in fatigues stood in the arched opening of the cave looking down at us. His hand hovered tensely near his hip, as if he was prepared to go for the gun that was strapped across his chest. Terrified, I reached over and dug my fingers into Mason's arm.

Mason noticed my expression and looked up at the opening of the cave. "It's okay," he whispered as the guy disappeared into the darkness again. Mason didn't seem surprised, so the guy must have been his bodyguard. But he did seem tense all of a sudden. "We should probably get back," he said to all of us. "It gets dark really fast once the sun sets behind the mountain."

It didn't take any convincing for everyone to agree. By the time we emerged out of the cave into the forest, the sun had dropped close to the crest of the mountain. Mason and Orrett made us jog down the trail to the dirt road because they knew it was going to get dark before we made it back to the village if we didn't hurry. Sophie swore the whole way.

Unlike the previous night, the sky was clear, so I said, "We can walk. It's not cloudy and the moon is almost full."

None of them slowed down, despite my comment. So, I hurried to keep up. When we entered the village, the moon cast a soft white glow on the people walking towards the mess tent for dinner. Sophie and I walked in front of the guys and a hand slid across my butt.

"Hey." I turned around to glare at Mason. "Did you just touch my ass?"

"No." He held his hands up in surrender. "Not exactly. You had a bug on the pocket of your shorts."

"Oh, really?"

"You did." He laughed. "It was one of those big rainbow-beetle things that fly and bite." He turned to Orrett for support. "Tell her that she had a bug on her butt."

"Don't try to drag me into this," Orrett protested. "I wasn't looking at Derian's derriere. I'm a married man."

I pointed at Mason in a mock threat, "Mason Cartwright, for the millionth time, I have a boyfriend. If you try any more funny business I'll call him on that crappy outer-space phone of yours and he'll come down here to make you wish you kept your hands to yourself."

I thought Mason would laugh—I was joking—but he looked stunned. I was confused because I was pretty sure he knew I wouldn't actually call Trevor. Orrett seemed puzzled and Sophie's forehead creased with worry.

When I finally realized what I had done, I flung my hands up to cover my mouth—as if it would stop the words that had already come out. Obviously, it was too late. I had already blurted out his first and last name.

Chapter 14

My eyes darted around to calculate how many people might have heard me say Mason's full name. There were a few villagers talking to each other as they passed through the site. There were also groups of volunteers headed to the mess tent. No one seemed to be paying attention to us, but I panicked as I realized how many people could have potentially heard me.

Orrett looked at me, then Mason, and then back at me. His face angled as he put the pieces together in his head, then he spun around to see who might have heard.

"I'm so sorry," I mumbled through my hand and the brace, which were still pressed tightly against my lips.

"Don't worry about it," Mason said. "I trust Orrett and no one else probably heard." He draped his arm across my shoulder and acted as if nothing had happened. "Let's eat. I'm starved."

I twisted to look over Mason's arm at Sophie and Orrett. They both still seemed a little stunned and it took them a second before they snapped out of it and followed us to the mess tent.

We filled our trays and sat at a table with the nurse and another volunteer, who I didn't know. I couldn't even think of eating because I felt so sick with myself. I didn't say one word while they all ate because I was too afraid I would blurt out something else stupid. Mason acted the way he always did—as if it was no big deal that I had just blown his cover. Orrett and Sophie didn't actually say much either, so Mason talked to the nurse and the volunteer and told them about the ruins we visited.

"Are you feeling all right, Derian? You look a little pale," the nurse said.

I nodded and tried to force a smile. Fortunately, the nurse and the other volunteer finished their dinner and said good night, so I didn't have to attempt small talk. Once the four of us were alone, I thudded my head down on the table to try to make the tent stop spinning.

Sophie leaned over and hissed in my ear, "Get it together. You're making it worse."

I sat up and tried to pull myself together. Not showing my emotions on the outside was nearly impossible for me. I was the worst faker in the world, which was why I couldn't lie very well—or apparently keep a secret very well, either.

"Would you please relax," Mason said. "Nobody heard and I don't want you to be all tense for the rest of the time you're here."

"Even if someone did hear, it doesn't necessarily mean anything," Orrett added.

"Do you think someone heard?" I finally spoke.

Orrett shrugged. "There were a couple of old villagers behind Bill when you said it. But I don't know if they even speak English or if they would know the connection to that name."

Mason's expression changed. He didn't look nervous, just serious.

"You're sending mixed messages," I said to Mason. "Is it serious or not?"

He shrugged. "My dad insisted on an alias because he believed it could potentially be a problem. I'm not worried."

"What's in it for the villagers if they blow his cover?" Sophie asked Orrett.

"A drug cartel will give them a cut of the ransom for their

loyalty. Some of the older generation aren't that thrilled about gringos coming into the village and getting all up in their business, so it would also be a good way to scare us all off."

"What's a gringo?"

"A foreigner."

With my stomach churning from the guilt, I stood up to leave. "I need to go to bed."

Their chairs scraped as they got up to follow me. It would be entirely my fault if his dad was right, so my only hope was that Mason was right. There was nothing I could do to take it back and I couldn't have felt worse unless I called up the kidnappers myself and told them to come take Mason while he was sleeping.

The moon and the stars made it bright enough for me to see without a lantern as I made my way across the site towards the bathrooms. Sophie jogged to catch up with me and the guys waited outside. Sophie glanced sideways at me while we stood at the sinks. There were other women around, so I couldn't say anything. Once the other women left and we were alone, I splashed cold water on my face and started to cry.

"Nobody heard," Sophie tried to reassure me.

"They did. And it's not just that. My visions mean something bad is going to happen, maybe they were about Mason, not Trevor." I sat on the floor beside the sinks and hugged my knees into my chest. "I can't believe I'm such an idiot. He found something he really likes doing. He's happy and I ruined it. And to add icing to the cake, it's probably going to be the last thing he ever does."

"You're being a little overly dramatic, don't you think? It's just a stupid name. Nobody cares."

"Don't you watch the news?"

"No, not really."

"It's not a joke. We're in the Guerrero State."

"I have no idea what that means."

I was about to explain, but she lifted her hand up to stop me.

"And I don't want to know. He has security. If he's in any danger they'll make him leave. Having a breakdown over it isn't going to change anything, so suck it up."

"He was already in potential danger and now it's probable. How can you not be worried?"

"Worry doesn't fix things, it just makes you worried. Everybody here adores him. Nobody's going to let him get hurt."

"Okay, you're right," I said and got off the floor. "But I'm going to convince him to go back with us. That will make me feel better."

When we emerged from the bathrooms, Mason was gone. Orrett was leaning against the wall with his foot jammed up behind him.

"Where's Bill," I asked frantically.

"He'll be right back. He's just talking to someone." He turned his head away as if seeing someone cry was something he couldn't quite stomach. "Please don't do that. Everything's fine," he said as he ventured a glance at my face, then quickly looked away again.

"Sorry." I took a deep breath to pull myself together.

Mason appeared from around the corner, holding up a lantern. He took one look at me and pulled me in towards his chest. He held me so tightly I could hear his heart beating. Beating way too fast. He leaned back and ran his thumbs over my cheeks to wipe away the tears.

"Come on, I have to talk to you guys."

We all followed Mason to Sophie's and my tent. He opened the flap and followed the three of us in, then put the lantern on the floor. Sophie and I sat on my bed. Mason sat beside Orrett on Sophie's bed. Mason's relaxed demeanour from dinner was gone. His expression was completely serious and it scared me. He inhaled deeply and looked at each one of us individually, then ran his finger over the scar that cut through his eyebrow.

"We have to leave," he said and his jaw muscle twitched with tension. "It's just a precaution. Colin doesn't think anything will happen, but he wants us gone in case it does. They sent for a vehicle and it should be here in twenty minutes."

"Who's Colin?" Sophie asked.

"The head of security."

I sat up rigidly and clenched the edge of the bunk with my fingers. "What does Colin think might happen?"

"Nothing, as long as I'm not here."

"Shit," Orrett said. "Does he think one of the drug cartels already knows?"

"He just thinks it's better if the girls and I aren't here."

"We have guards," Sophie pointed out.

"Only two. The cartel guys will just shoot them," Orrett stated matter-of-factly.

"No," I squeaked pathetically.

"How do we know they won't hurt anyone else even if we're gone?" Sophie asked.

"We don't." Mason sighed heavily.

"We have to take Orrett with us too. He has a kid," Sophie insisted.

"I'm so sorry," I said, barely audible even to me.

Mason didn't say anything. He just closed his eyes and rested his head back on the side of the canvas tent.

"Are the local children in danger?" I asked.

Mason tilted his head forward and his eyes locked with mine. He didn't exactly answer my question. He simply said, "We have to leave."

I rested my elbows on my knees and banged my brace repeatedly against my forehead. It hurt, but I didn't care. I felt so stupid. All I had to do was call him Bill for a couple of days. Was that really so hard to do? Lives only depended on it. I felt like I should volunteer to be kidnapped and then refuse the ransom. I deserved whatever punishment they could dish out, especially if the children were harmed in any way. I wouldn't be able to live with myself if anyone was hurt because of my air-headed move.

I wanted Mason to yell at me and tell me I was an idiot or useless. I wanted him to say that he was disappointed in me, and that he hated me, and that he never wanted to see me again for as long as we lived.

He didn't yell at me. He leaned across the tent and hugged me. "It's not your fault, Derian. We're just leaving as a precaution. I should have never brought you here. It's my fault."

"You won't be able to come back. I ruined everything for you and you won't even have a chance to say good-bye to everyone." I held his hands. "Hector will be so sad that you had to leave."

Mason stared at the floor. Obviously, it hadn't occurred to him that he would be leaving behind people he cared about. After a while, he shook his head and said, "The project is almost finished. I would have been leaving soon anyway."

Sophie dropped to her knees and stuffed her clothes into her bag. "Derian, get packed."

"We can worry now?" I snapped. She shot me a vicious look, so I threw my things into my bag, then looked at Orrett. "I'm sorry I screwed everything up for you too."

"It's just a precaution for Ritchie Rich here." He chuckled. "I live in a bungalow in Whittier. Nobody's going to want to hold me for ransom."

"I'd feel better if you came along too," Mason said.

"Nah. I'm going home in another week anyway and I've got a few root canals to do before then." Orrett shook Mason's hand and hugged him over one shoulder. "Take care, man."

"I'll call you when you're back in LA," Mason said.

"You better come for a visit. The wife wants to have you over for dinner. I'm not sure what to call you anymore, but we'll worry about that later. Ladies, it's been a pleasure. Be safe." Orrett hugged Sophie and me. "Oh, I should get you some painkillers to take with you. Let me run to the medical tent. I'll be right back."

Orrett opened the flap to our tent and stepped outside. I glanced up at Mason to check his expression. He forced a smile before I had a chance to figure out how he was really feeling.

"Mason, you need to pack your things too."

"Yeah." He shook his head like he was trying to clear a fog and make his brain think straight. "I don't have that much stuff here, nothing I need, anyway."

"What about Hector's wind chime? We have to take that with us, and the letters you wrote me. I want to read the letters. Go to your tent and we'll meet you there when we're done."

"Uh." He paused and ran his hand through his hair. "It's okay. I'll wait for you to finish and we can all walk over together."

"Why don't you want us to walk by ourselves?"

His forehead was shiny with sweat. "I don't mind waiting."

He avoided looking at me, so I stopped what I was doing and stood to face him. I had to hold his chin to force him to look at me. The expression in his eyes gave him away. "You're afraid to leave us alone, aren't you?"

He didn't say anything.

"I thought you said it was just a precaution."

"A necessary precaution."

Sophie stood up straight and pushed him in the chest. "What the hell is that supposed to mean?"

"It means we have to leave. All right?" His voice rose with the stress of the situation. I had never seen him rattled before and it was extremely unsettling.

Sophie and I quickly zipped our bags as Orrett poked his head back in the tent. He handed me a plastic Ziploc bag of pills. "Here are your painkillers."

"Thanks." I stuffed them into my pocket.

"Looks like your transportation is already here," he said as he looked back over his shoulder.

We climbed out of the tent. The headlights of four vehicles lit up the area as they skidded into camp. Mason and Orrett both stepped in front of us. I peered around them as men filed out of the four trucks. Several locals from the village took off running. My body tensed and the hairs on the back of my neck stood up as one of the men from the trucks pushed two volunteers to the ground. A gasping sound escaped my throat when the guy pressed the long barrel of a gun into the back of another volunteer. The volunteer laced his hands behind his head and dropped to his knees as he followed directions I couldn't hear.

My body froze in place. I didn't even flinch when the bodyguard who I'd seen earlier at the cave jumped out from behind the tent to stand between us and the vehicles. His stance was wide and his gun was drawn. I watched in shock as our two other armed guards took positions against the corners of tent frames and also pointed their guns towards the headlights.

Mason turned to Sophie and me and yelled, "Run!"

He said it with so much intensity it startled me. I dropped my bag as Sophie grabbed my hand and pulled me towards the forest. I yanked my hand out of her grasp, turned, and ran back to Mason. "I'm not leaving without you."

"Run!" He shouted louder and the tendons in his neck stretched tightly.

I dug my fingers into his arm and tried to pull him as a spotlight scanned across the camp. It lit up Orrett and Mason's bodyguard.

"Derian, they will kill you. Run!" Mason pushed me so hard the force almost made me fall down.

"Not without you!" I shouted.

Several flashes blew out of the barrel of the gun. Orrett's body jolted backwards. My instinct was to try to catch him, but my nervous system wasn't responding. I watched helplessly as he slumped to the ground and lay motionlessly. Mason's bodyguard shouted, "Go! Go! Go!," as he and the other guards returned fire.

Mason grabbed my hand and we both sprinted into the forest behind Sophie.

Chapter 15

The sound of gunfire cracked through the air and made me flinch and cringe repeatedly as the bullets hit trees around us. The moonlight was filtered by the treetops, so I couldn't see that well. I kept falling and landing on my brace. Sophie must have been falling too because I could hear her groan and swear. We were definitely being followed. And it was impossible to tell if it was the security guards or the gunmen. Their footsteps and heavy breathing got louder as they gained on us. I was too afraid to slow down to look over my shoulder. But when I heard them speaking Spanish I knew for sure they were the men from the trucks. My stomach sank and collapsed on itself as I realized it probably meant the guards had gone down. I ran faster.

Mason and I caught up to Sophie and I passed her to take the lead. Trevor and I had spent our entire childhood climbing in the forested mountains around Britannia Beach, so I was used to the terrain, but not in the dark. I scrambled over rocks and hopped fallen tree trunks, stumbling almost every fifth stride. Branches slashed my arms and legs as we moved through the dense bush. Mason passed me and stomped through the vegetation to make a path for us. Unfortunately, it was also making it easier for our pursuers. They gained more ground, moving fast—

faster than even Trevor could travel. We were so screwed. We reached an opening in the woods and I pulled Sophie and Mason's hands. "This way." We sprinted along the edge of the clearing, where it was easier to run.

When we reached the other side, Sophie whimpered then fell to her knees. "Go without me."

"No." I stopped and turned to help her. Mason had already pulled her to her feet. I glanced back. I couldn't see the men, but I knew they were standing in the middle of the clearing because I could hear them talking. "Shh," I breathed out. Sophie and Mason both turned to see what I was looking at. "It's too dark for them to see us. They can only hear us. If we stay still, they might leave."

We all stood perfectly motionless in the shadows of the trees. I tried to slow my breathing to make it quieter, but the best I could do was an erratic wheeze. One of the men shouted something in Spanish. I saw a flash before I heard the crack of a gunshot that was aimed in our direction.

"They have night scopes," Mason said and shoved us to keep going. We ducked into the forest and started running again. Bullets whizzed by us. One hit the tree right in front of me and the splinters of bark sprayed into my face. It was surreal—like one of my visions, only it was really happening. My muscles burned, my lungs protested with each expansion, and my skin scraped with every fall. Sophie was crying. I turned left and led us uphill, hoping the men would assume we would take the easier downhill route.

As we got higher out of the canopy of the big trees, it was a bit easier to see. I ran along a rocky ridge and turned to reach my hand out for Sophie. We scrambled up a rounded rock mass that overlooked a valley. It was too dark to tell what would be the best escape route.

"I need to stop," Sophie gasped and rested her hands on her knees.

"We can't." I pulled her by the elbow.

She yanked her arm out of my grasp. "I can't. Go without me."

"We're not leaving you here," Mason said as he checked over his shoulder. "I think we can rest for a second. I can't hear them."

"How long do you think we've been running?" Sophie asked.

Mason said, "Probably forty-five minutes."

I knew it had been longer because of where the moon had risen to, probably more like two hours. I searched the sky for a star to follow—that's what Trevor would have told me to do—not that he was experienced with being chased by men with guns. Tears ran down my face as I thought about Trevor. He was going to be so mad at me. If he were with us, he'd be yelling at me for putting myself and everyone else in so much danger. Actually, if he were with me, none of it would have happened in the first place.

"We have to at least keep walking," I whispered and headed in the direction of the star.

As we walked, I listened for the sound of the men following us. I was also trying to detect the sound of water. Trevor always told me that if I was lost in the forest I could follow the water downhill. There was no running water, the dense ground brush was impossible to move through quickly, and I couldn't see worth shit. I stopped in a heavily wooded area and bent over to puke.

"We're going to die," I choked out between heaves.

"No we're not," Mason said, without much conviction. "We're going to be okay."

Sophie stood with her hands on her hips trying to catch her breath. "Maybe we should dig a hole and hide under the mulch."

"They're still too close. We don't have time," I whispered.

The light of a flashlight scanned across the trees we were standing behind. We all froze. I held my breath. A man's voice yelled something in Spanish. Sophie and I both looked at Mason for an interpretation.

"Run!" he shouted.

We took off again and zig-zagged through the trees. We scrambled up a rocky incline on an angle to make the climb less steep and I heard the distinct rumbling of running water. It was coming from the other side of a ridge—a huge ridge. Another bullet ricocheted right next to me and sent slate shrapnel flying all around us. Once we cleared the top of the ridge, I dug my heels into the dirt to climb down the slope. I literally had to skid to a stop when I realized I was about to fall over a cliff. The loose dirt slid under my feet and I landed on my butt. Sophie and Mason caught up to me and stared over the edge as I scrambled back to a standing position. We were at the top of a waterfall, which was over fifty feet high. I could only sort of see the river at the bottom in the slivers of moonlight. It was impossible to tell if it was deep enough to jump or if there were rocks under the surface.

"We have to go back," Mason urged us.

We turned and saw four flashlights bouncing through the forest towards us. "Your dad will pay the ransom. Why don't we just give up? He'll pay them and then they'll release us," Sophie reasoned.

"It doesn't work that way here," Mason muttered under his breath. "They'll take the ransom and kill us anyway—or worse."

I grabbed Mason's hand with the fingers on my braced hand and Sophie's hand with my good hand, then turned around. "We can jump. I saw this in a vision. We're going to be fine if we jump." I pulled and felt resistance from both of them.

"No way," Sophie scoffed.

"We have no choice."

"I can't," Sophie cried.

Shots rang through the night air and bullets skimmed by dangerously close to my head. "Trust me. I saw it in a vision. It's going to be okay—I think." I pulled them again and we all ran three steps, then leapt over the edge.

Chapter 16

I had no idea if we were going to make it. My visions hadn't really extended past the hitting-the-water part. The air tore past my ears as we fell. It was just like what I had seen in my vision. I was falling and falling. It seemed to take forever and my body instinctively flailed as it realized the height I had just flung it from. Every one of my muscles clenched at the thought of making impact with something completely unknown. I had way too much time to think about what was going to happen. My dying wish was to kiss Trevor one last time.

My hand slipped from Mason's and he hit the water first. Then I was driven under water and separated from Sophie. There was a delay in the agonizing pain that shot through my body from the impact of the water. It felt like something ripped through my tissues, then shattered my bones. The pressure of the water on my skull was intense. It was too dark to see Sophie or Mason. I couldn't tell which way was up but I kicked hard and propelled myself in the direction that I hoped was the surface. My lungs moved inside my chest, expecting oxygen, and I had the unbearable urge to take a breath. I couldn't remember if drowning was supposed to be a good or a bad way to die. It seemed like a bad way to me. I was about to give up and take a breath of water when arms wrapped around my chest and pulled. After I broke through the surface, I gasped repeatedly to fill my lungs over and over.

Mason dove back down and resurfaced only seconds later with Sophie. "Are you okay?" he asked her.

She nodded and gasped.

He swam over to me and asked the same thing, "Are you okay?"

"I think so. Are you?"

"I'm fine. What else did you see in your vision?"

"Nothing. It ended here."

He looked up at the top of the waterfall. I followed his gaze and saw the silhouettes of the four men. They shot down at us.

"Dive!" I screamed.

I dove under the surface and swam towards a pile of large rocks near the far bank of the river. The brace on my wrist made it hard to swim effectively, so Sophie and Mason made it to the shore before I did. We slinked out of the water and crept behind the rocks. I crouched down next to Sophie and listened for more gun shots. I was shaking so badly it felt like a seizure. I couldn't make it stop. Mason peered over the rocks. "They're on the move. We have to keep going," he said and pulled us both to our feet.

"I can't." I stumbled to the ground.

Mason yanked one of my arms and Sophie pushed my butt to get me going. I tried to jog, but my legs were ridiculously weak. I stumbled again, then tried to walk—it was more of a drunken stagger. My brace felt slimy-wet against my skin, so I took it off and shoved it down the back waistband of my shorts. I fell and landed on my wrist that no longer had the brace on it. I expected it to do some damage, and I waited for the pain, but it never came. I felt nothing. I was strangely numb. The trees around me moved in a wave, as if the ground was a waterbed. My eyes tried desperately to focus, but every blink made my vision blur again. Something was wrong. I rested on my hands and knees, digging my fingers into the grainy dirt to try to make the ground stay still. It was difficult to tell if the men were behind us because all I could hear was a horrible gasping sound. It took a second for me to figure out that the sound was my own breathing. I blinked repeatedly and tried to snap my head out of the weird fog.

"Mason!" Sophie yelled. She ran back and crouched next to me.

I heard Mason's footsteps run back to where we were. It sounded like he gasped. "What is that?"

"She's hurt," Sophie said frantically.

I tried to say I was fine, but only a muffled gurgling sound came out of my throat. Then I tasted blood.

"Derian, you're hurt."

"Her shirt is soaked in blood."

I struggled to look over my shoulder and got extremely dizzy. My shirt had changed a dark colour all the way down my back. I collapsed down onto my stomach and rested my cheek on the ground.

Dad, I screwed up real bad. I think I got shot, I'm lost, and I can't run anymore. It's okay if I die because I'll come to be with you, but please help Sophie and Mason. I love you and I'm sorry that I messed up so badly.

My eyesight focused in and out. Mason took his shirt off and folded it up to pad my back wound. Sophie slid her belt off and they angled it across my shoulder and under my armpit to hold his shirt in place. His shirt was completely soaked in blood before they even finished tightening the belt. Mason pressed both his hands down on my back to try to stop the bleeding. His arms trembled as he held the pressure. The dirt scratched against my cheek and all I could hear was my own raspy breathing. Everything turned black and even the sound of my breathing went silent.

When I opened my eyes, I watched Sophie take her shirt off. She layered it on top of Mason's, then tightened the belt again.

They fitted my brace back on my wrist. The forest floor spun like the Tilt-a-Whirl at the fair. I spread my arms out as if I were flying and tried to hold on as the ground rotated beneath me.

When I became aware again, I was sitting up with Mason crouched beside me. "Where are we?"

"Mexico." Mason pulled my arm to slide me onto his back. He hooked his elbows under my knees to prop me up in a piggyback. He was breathing heavily and his chest expanded against me. "Hold on, Deri. Don't you dare let go."

"Am I going to die?"

"No."

"I think I'm going to die. Promise you won't blame yourself," I breathed out.

"I will blame myself, so you better hold on."

"No. Blame me."

My brain transitioned in and out of blackness. Each time I opened my eyes, Mason was still carrying me on his back. Sophie was leading us along the river. I couldn't tell how much time had passed between blackouts. It felt like a long time. Eventually, I couldn't tell anything.

"Deri, try to stay awake," Mason said and I felt his fingers pinch my leg.

"But I'm sleepy."

"Try to stay awake so you can hold on. I can't carry you if you let go." My eyelids closed. I tried desperately to open them again, but they weighed a ton. They were jarred open when I hit the ground. "Sorry, Deri." Mason must have slid me off his back to take a rest. He kneeled next to me and cradled my head onto his lap. Sophie cupped her hands and scooped water out of the stream, then tipped it into my mouth.

"Where are we?" I mumbled. "I should get back to the Inn. Granddad is going to wonder where I went."

"We'll be there soon."

"I'm tired. Can you carry me?"

"Sure."

"Where's Trevor?"

"He's going to be at the Inn when we get there."

"Okay. I'm thirsty."

Sophie scooped more water and tipped it for me to drink, then everything went dark again. The next thing I remembered was riding on Mason's back, my chin propped on his shoulder and my teeth clanking against each other with each step he took. My eyes kept trying to stay closed, but I fought after each blink to pry them open. I could tell it was night and we were in a forest, but I couldn't remember why.

"Are you Mason?"

"Yes."

"I don't want you to get hurt."

"I know."

"Am I hurt?"

"You're going to be okay."

"Bill."

"Yes."

"That's what I'm supposed to call you, right?"

"It's okay now."

"Are you mad at me?"

"No."

"You should be." I tilted my head so my cheek rested on his shoulder and then closed my eyes.

Dad, can you please help Mason and Sophie find a safe place to rest? I'll probably see you soon. I love you.

Chapter 17

The sky brightened as dawn arrived. I vaguely remembered leaving the camp before bed time and travelling through the forest all night, but I didn't understand why we would have done that. Mason slid me gently off his back. We were in some sort of small cave and I could hear the stream rushing outside. Mason stepped near the opening of the cave. Silhouetted with the filtered morning sunlight in the background, he looked like he used to in my dreams. My eyes got heavy and the next time I opened them, he was kneeling next to me. He tipped a huge, green, waxy leaf up towards my lips. The cool water rolled forward on the leaf and I forgot to tell my mouth to open, so it ran down my jaw. He tipped the leaf back for a second, then tried again. I was able to split my lips open just enough to let the water trickle in. My eyes closed and I saw my dad. He was standing in the snow. He seemed worried.

"Is something wrong?" I asked Sophie before she tipped a leaf full of water towards my mouth.

"Just drink."

"Okay." My throat didn't open and the water choked me. "Are we in Britannia Beach?"

"Almost."

My hands shook so bad it seemed as if I had a tremor. When

I looked back up at Sophie, everything went dark. "I can't see you. Where did you go?"

"I'm right here." I felt her hand on mine.

"Why can't I see you?"

"You're just tired, Deri."

"Can you tell Trevor to come here?"

"Yeah."

The wound burned with a radiating throb that expanded over more and more of my back with each passing minute. It felt like someone had heated up a fireplace poker until it was white hot, then drove it into my body and twisted it around. Mason sat with me propped up in his lap. His arms wrapped around me to keep me warm.

"My dad is here. He's with Cody. Do you want to meet him?"

Mason kissed my forehead. "Not right now, Deri. Tell him I'll meet him some other time. Not right now."

"Okay. What happened?"

"Don't worry about anything right now. Just concentrate on getting better."

"I'm shot."

"You're going to be okay."

"But, they shot Orrett, right?"

"He's going to be okay, too."

"Did they shoot him because I called you Mason?"

"No. They shot him because I am Mason."

"Are we in Mexico?"

"Just rest, Deri."

"Okay."

Dad, what if I don't get to be where you are? What if I can't be with you because of the bad thing I did? I think people are dead because of what I did. It's bad. Really bad. I might not be forgiven. Obviously, I don't deserve to be with you. That's my punishment. I'm sorry if that hurts you. Maybe it doesn't. I must be a colossal disappointment to you.

The damp floor of the cave dug into the bony parts of my shoulder blades and hips, but moving caused excruciating pain in my back, so I endured the discomfort. I wanted to whimper, but since I was starting to remember that it was entirely my fault, I wouldn't let myself. I was glad I was the one who was going to die. I deserved to suffer and I was glad it was taking painfully long. I could feel a hand holding mine. It was rough and strong and it felt so familiar.

"Trevor?" I smiled. "Please keep Mason and Sophie safe. Sorry I screwed up."

The hand moved and ran down the contour of my face. I fell asleep.

When I opened my eyes, it was getting dark again outside the cave, so at least one day had gone by. I turned my head to see who was holding me. It was Mason. "Where did Trevor go?"

"Uh, he'll be back soon." Mason rested his palm on my forehead as if he was checking my temperature. "He's getting you some more water. He wants you to drink more water so you'll get stronger."

"Okay."

I closed my eyes and dreamed about Trevor when he was old. He had children who were grown and their families were visiting for a summer barbecue in the back yard. One of his grandsons, who looked just like Trevor, asked Trevor to tell him his best rescue story. Trevor told him about the time he had to fly all the way to Mexico to try to save someone from men with guns. The grandkids all thought he was making it up.

I woke up from the dream and felt the dampness of the cave soaking into my skin. Sophie and Mason talked near the opening. He was shirtless and she was just wearing a bra and shorts, so obviously their shirts were still acting as gauze for my bullet hole. I tried to shout out to them. It came out like a husky whisper, "Tell Trevor to come back inside. I'm cold."

Mason turned and walked over. He cradled me and moved

me to a spot where the sun was angling into the cave, then he knelt and slid in next to me. He whispered in my ear, "Trevor's looking for a way to get us out of here. I'll keep you warm until he gets back."

"Okay."

When I woke up again, I knew Trevor was back. I could feel the side of my face resting on his warm chest. I could hear his heart beating and it made me feel safe. When he felt me move, he wrapped his arms even tighter around me.

"Trevor, I'm going to die. Will you be able to forgive me?"

"No," he whispered almost inaudibly.

"Did you find a way to get Mason and Sophie home?"

He kissed the top of my head, but didn't say anything. I wasn't sure if he was reassuring me that he would get them home soon, or if he was consoling me because that wasn't going to happen.

"I'm glad you're here." I tilted my head up and pressed my lips against his. It felt so good to kiss him again, almost like the first time. It felt as if electricity was pulsating through my body and it made me feel better.

The next time I woke up, Mason was sitting with me again. He looked tense and concerned.

"Hey." I smiled and my lips cracked from the dryness. "Don't look so worried. Trevor will get you out of here. He won't quit until you're safe. I promise."

Mason forced a smile. "Trevor wants you to get stronger so we can all go home. Can you do that for him?"

I nodded.

"Do you still have the Tylenol 3s Orrett gave you?"

"Maybe in my pocket."

Mason reached into my pocket and pulled out the plastic bag. He placed two in my mouth and tipped some water from a leaf in so I could swallow. I closed my eyes and concentrated very hard on healing my body because Trevor wanted me to. I imagined an army of little workers rushing around inside me. I pretended they were repairing everything that needed to be fixed. They cleaned and rebuilt all of my internal organs and tissues. It was kind of cute and funny. When they discovered the bullet wound, they all looked up at it like a meteor had created a big gaping hole in the ceiling. They each comically scratched their heads in bewilderment.

Sophie woke me up to drink more water from the leaf.

"Does Trevor think we can leave soon?" I asked her.

Her eyebrows angled together, her forehead creased, and her lips formed into her sympathetic pout. "Soon," she said.

I faded in and out of sleep, or maybe it was consciousness. I lost track of how many times the sun had come and gone outside of the little cave. My dreams were crazy and didn't make any sense. Sometimes, there were people who I didn't even know in my dreams. Other times it was Sophie, Mason, and me. The three of us were sailing in a boat in the middle of the ocean and we realized there was a hole in the hull and we were taking on water. Sophie and Mason tried to bail the water out with big leaves, but it was filling the boat faster than they could scoop it out. I woke up all sweaty and breathing heavy.

By the following afternoon, I was able to sit up on my own and I was feeling a little bit better. Sophie helped me stand and walked me down to get cleaned up with the stream water.

"How many days have we been here?"

"Two," she said as she helped me to sit on the shore with my back to the water. She reclined me and splashed water over my hair.

"That's it? Trevor got here so quickly. How long did it take him to find us?"

Sophie didn't answer. She cupped her hands to splash water over the rest of my hair.

"Sophie. How long has Trevor been here?"

She sighed, sat me back up, and moved to sit down on the

dirt. She rested her elbows on her knees and looked at me with the most pitiful expression. "Trevor's not here. You were just imagining him."

"What?" I stood up but got dizzy and fell to my knees next to the stream. "No. He was here. He came for us. I know he did."

"You were delirious. You only imagined him."

"No." I sat on my knees for a long time, staring out at the trees. "I was talking to him."

"No. You thought you were talking to him."

I folded my hands together and rested my forehead on them. I was pretty sure God only answered prayers for people who went to church, but I wanted to pray. I needed to.

"Dear God, please help Trevor to find us. I know he's looking and I know he won't stop until he finds us. Please guide him in the right direction and keep him safe. I know I have no right to ask You for any favours, but Trevor does and he's going to try, whether You help him or not. Thank you."

I looked over at Sophie and she smiled with sadness in her eyes. "Let's finish getting you cleaned up."

"Do you think God will answer my prayer?"

"Yes."

I stripped down to my underwear, took my brace off, and stepped into the water. I dunked down just far enough to keep the bullet wound out of the water. I felt better for about two minutes before I remembered something that brought all of my hopes crashing down. My heart sunk into a heavy puddle in the bottom of my chest as I realized that my prayer wasn't going to be answered. My visions had all been about Trevor being lost and never finding me.

I looked over at Sophie, who was swimming in the water. She didn't notice that I was on the verge of freaking out. I held my hands under the water so it wouldn't be obvious how badly they were shaking. I didn't know if I felt more like crying or swearing. The whole reason I told Trevor not to go on any rescues was because I knew all along that he was going to fail. I just didn't know it was me he was going to fail to find. The worst part was I knew he was going to try anyway. He was going to be devastated that he couldn't rescue us.

"Do you think the cartel guys are still out there?" I asked.

She shrugged. "We heard some voices not far away yesterday afternoon, but they were too far away to tell what they were saying or who they were."

I finished washing, climbed out of the water, and sat in the sun next to my clothes. My legs were shaking, so I hugged my arms around my knees to keep them still. The ring Trevor gave me sparkled in the sunshine. I stared at it as I spun it around and around on my finger.

"Mason and I think his dad has probably sent someone out to search for us."

"I don't think they'll find us."

"Why?"

"In my vision Trevor was lost and couldn't find us. I think it means we're screwed unless we get out of here on our own."

"Great." She waded out of the water and passed Mason on her way up to the cave.

He walked down and sat next to me on a rock. "Everything okay?"

I sighed and kicked the water. "Trevor doesn't know we're lost, and even if he did, he wouldn't know where to start to look for us."

"My dad will know that I went missing with you. They'll figure it out. Someone will find us."

"You think?"

"Sure. They've probably already sent a team out searching." He sighed. "Unless the drug cartel stayed at the camp and prevented the volunteers from contacting my dad."

"So, it's possible that no one outside the camp knows what happened?"

"It's possible." He stood as if he was in pain and tried unsuccessfully to straighten his leg.

"What's wrong?"

"The knee I had surgery on swells a little when I run too much on it."

"A little?" I waded out of the water and followed him onto shore, then reached over to place my palm on his leg. "It's the size of a cantaloupe, and hot. You need to soak it in the stream."

"I have been. It doesn't hurt. Now that you're feeling a bit better, I'll carry you again."

"You can't carry me if your knee is that swollen." I sighed and closed my eyes to help me think. "I'm almost strong enough to walk. We can make our way down the mountain. All we have to do is find the main road or a village."

"We have no food. You're only going to get weaker. We're all going to get weaker."

"We don't need food for a while. We'll be fine as long as we have water."

"Yeah? Did you see that in a vision?"

"No."

He turned slightly when I said that, and I noticed he also had an injury.

"Mason! Your arm."

"It's fine. The bullet only grazed it."

I examined the wound close up. "It's still bleeding."

"Again? Shit. It won't stop, for some reason. It's not even that bad." He tore a leaf off a nearby tree and applied it with pressure on his arm.

"Here, let me." I stood and moved his hand away so I could use both my hands to apply pressure.

"I can't even tell you how sorry I am that I put you guys in danger. I want you to hate me," he said and winced from the pain.

"That's not possible. Besides, it's my fault we're in danger. I want you to hate me."

"That's not possible."

I tipped my head up to meet his eyes. They had turned the darker shade of blue that only happened when he was sad. I suddenly remembered I had kissed someone when I thought Trevor was sitting with me in the cave. "Did I kiss you?"

He stared at me for a while, licked his bottom lip, and said, "No."

"That's good," I said, even though I knew he lied. "I don't want to complicate things."

"Yeah, things are pretty complicated already."

"Do you think Orrett is—?"

"I don't know. Let's not worry about any of that." He stretched his arm across my shoulder and pulled me in for a hug. "Let's just worry about getting out of here alive. Nothing else matters right now."

Chapter 18

Time went really slowly after I became more alert. My shoulder was killing me and my stomach felt raw on the inside from the hunger. None of us really talked because there wasn't anything to say. When it got dark on the third night, I said, "You guys should go down the mountain together tomorrow. I'll stay here."

"I'm not leaving you," Mason said.

"I don't think I'm strong enough to walk yet and you won't be able to carry me." I pointed at his knee that had swelled to the size of a watermelon.

"I'm not leaving you," he repeated.

"Mason. Be reasonable. If you guys don't go get help, we're all going to die."

Sophie didn't say anything, but she shifted the position she was sitting in.

I could tell Mason wasn't going to budge his opinion, so I said, "Maybe I'll feel well enough in the morning to come with you." Then I let it go.

Mason got up and disappeared outside the cave.

"You'll have to go by yourself if he refuses," I whispered to Sophie.

"I don't know if I can do it alone."

"You can."

"If we stay here, someone will eventually find us."

"We'll need food before that happens. Mason can't carry me and I don't think I can make it."

She started to cry.

"Sophie, you're the strongest female I've ever met. You can do it."

"Haven't you known me long enough to realize that the tough-girl thing is all just a big act?"

"You can do it," I repeated.

Mason came back into the cave. It was too dark to see him, but I felt the warmth of his body when he slid down to lie next to me. His breathing was initially shallow, then slowed and got deeper. It almost sounded as if he'd fallen asleep until something crashed through the bushes outside. Mason sat up. Sophie made a whimpering sound and scooted closer to me. We all held our breath and listened. It was moving around close to the opening of the cave.

I reached through the darkness and searched for Mason's hand. When I found it, he tightened his fingers around mine. We sat perfectly still. I could hear a sniffing sound, sort of like what a black bear in Britannia Beach would sound like if it was searching for food. "It's an animal. Make noise," I said as I stood up and clapped. "Ha! Ha! Get!"

Mason stood and clapped his hands. "Yeah! Yeah!"

"What are you doing?" Sophie whimpered. "Don't tell it we're here."

"It already knows. It can smell us. Ha! Get!" I stomped my feet and yelled some more. Then I listened. The bushes rustled as it ran away.

"What do you think it was?" Sophie asked, from a safe position behind Mason.

"I don't know. It was big, though," I said.

"It was most likely a coyote."

"Are there still jaguars around here?"

"I don't know. The locals have lots of legends, but it's hard to know what's true and what's not. I'm sure it was just a coyote."

"What if it comes back?" Sophie asked.

"I'll stay awake," Mason offered as he sat down near the opening of the cave.

"We'll take shifts," I said. "Wake me up when you get tired."

In the morning, my stomach growled painfully to remind me that I hadn't eaten in days. I should have never complained about the food at the camp. If I'd known it was the last thing I was ever going to eat, I would have tried to appreciate it a little more. There were a lot of things I would have tried to appreciate more.

I rolled over. Sophie was asleep beside me. Mason was still sitting awake near the opening. "You didn't wake me," I said to him.

"I didn't get tired." He turned his head to look at me.

I got up and rested my hand briefly on his shoulder as I passed. "I have to use the facilities. I'll be right back."

I wandered out of the cave on my own. My legs were still weak and my steps were pathetically unstable. After I peed, I carefully walked down the shore for a few metres, searching for berries. Trevor had taught me the difference between edible and poisonous berries at home, but I wasn't sure if it was the same in Mexico. It didn't matter because I didn't find any berry bushes anyway. I considered catching a fish, and I would have, if there had been any fish in the stream. I decided that snagging a bird or a lizard would be a good option, especially if I started a fire to cook it with. Then I realized it might not be a good idea to have a fire in case the drug-cartel guys were still after us.

I crouched down at the edge of the water and put two pain-killers on my tongue then cupped my hands to scoop some water into my mouth. I scooped another handful to splash over my face and I heard a noise. It sounded like something walking up behind me. I tried to spin around and stand up at the same time, but fell to my butt.

"Graceful," Sophie snickered.

"You scared me."

"Sorry."

I moved to sit on a flat stone near the edge of the water. She crouched down to cup water. She drank a few handfuls, then climbed up and sat next to me on the rock. I hugged her. "I'm sorry I got us into this mess and that I haven't been a great friend lately. I feel horrible that I didn't know about Doug or your plans to go back to school."

"You're the best friend I could ask for, Deri." She sighed and looked up at the trees. "I talked you into coming here, remember? And the reason I didn't tell you about Doug was because I knew you would talk me out of it. The reason I didn't tell you about wanting to be a teacher was because I knew you would talk me into it."

"I don't want you to avoid telling me things because you're worried I would pressure you. I'll support you no matter what you do or don't want to do. It's your life, not mine."

After a long, heavy pause, she said, "I made a mistake with Doug."

"You can fix it when you see him again."

"If."

"No. When." I noticed she was wearing the ring Doug had given her when she graduated. "He's going to be excited to work it out."

"Our lives have gone in different directions. I don't think it can work if he's going to keep touring."

"You didn't even try."

"I don't need to try some things to know they're going to end up a disaster."

"You guys have something special. You shouldn't throw it away without trying everything."

She sighed and nodded.

I pointed at her feet. "My adorable canvas slip-ons have taken quite a beating."

"Yeah, I owe you a new pair." She threw stones in the stream. "Are we going to try to make it down the mountain today?"

"Yeah, I think I can do it. All we have to do is find a road or a village. I don't think it will be that hard."

"What if we run into the drug dealers?"

"I don't know. We can't stay here forever, though. We'll need food eventually. We could risk a fire and have some barbecued snake if you want."

"Ha. I think I'd rather starve, but ask me again tomorrow."

I stretched my arm around her shoulders and squeezed tightly. "I'm glad you're with me. I'm sorry I dragged you into this mess, but I wouldn't be able to get through this if you weren't here with me."

She made a face and flicked my arm. "Ya, there's no one I would rather be running for my life with than you."

I chuckled. "Do you think your dad will let you go on vacation with me again?"

"If we don't tell him what happened."

"Okay. Here's the plan, we'll walk down to the road, hook up with a ride back to the resort, and get on a plane back to Vancouver. He won't even know. It's brilliant."

"You are shot, though," she pointed out. "Someone might ask how that happened."

I laughed. "True."

"I've got an idea. We'll tell everyone we went snorkelling and a stingray stabbed you with its tail."

"I like it."

We both turned to look over our shoulders when we heard footsteps coming up behind us. "Morning, ladies," Mason said. "Are you enjoying your Mexican vacation?"

"The bed is a little hard and the food sucks, but other than that I would give it rave revues," I said.

He waded into the water to wash up. He dunked completely under the surface and pushed his wet hair back off his face, then stood frozen in the water and searched the sky. A second later, I heard what he heard.

"It's a helicopter." I pulled Mason and Sophie's t-shirts out from under the belt tourniquet over my shoulder. "Here, tear this along the side seam." I handed Mason his shirt. "We have to lay the fabric out on top of a tree so they can see us from the air."

"What if it's the cartel guys?" Mason asked.

I looked up at the sky and considered our options. "It could be one of your dad's, or military, or even commercial. The odds are in our favour. Do you think you can climb that tree and spread the fabric over the top branches?"

"They're circling around," Sophie said. "They're searching along the stream. What if it's the cartel guys and we end up showing them exactly where we are?"

I pointed downstream about fifty metres to a group of shorter trees that weren't as crowded by taller trees. "We have to take that chance. We'll put the signal there. They can't land the helicopter here anyway. They'll have to hike in. If the cartel guys show up, we'll see them before they see us. It will give us enough time to run and hide."

Mason ran down the pebble shore and climbed one of the taller trees. When he got as close to the top as he could, he flung the t-shirts across the top of the branches next to him. He scanned the sky for a while, then shouted, "I think they're going the other way."

Sophie and I stared up at the sky as well. I couldn't even hear the helicopter anymore. Mason started to climb down one branch at a time and when he was about ten feet off the ground, the branch he stepped on snapped. He fell the rest of the way and landed awkwardly.

"Shit," he moaned and held his knee into his chest.

Sophie ran to him. I rushed as quickly as I could, but my

legs were not cooperating and I kept stumbling. She reached him and knelt down. He groaned in pain, but it sounded as if he was trying to stifle it. I eventually got to them and helped him sit up.

"I'm okay," he strained to say. The tendons in his neck stretched tightly and his jaw didn't move as he spoke through clenched teeth. He sucked in a deep breath and exhaled slowly, as if he was bracing for pain.

I glanced at Sophie, concerned.

"I think the helicopter went south," Mason said. He winced as he tried to straighten his leg. It wouldn't extend, so he gave up trying and left it bent.

"Can you walk?"

"Yeah." He tried to get up, but fell back on his butt.

Sophie frowned, then tilted her face up at the sky. "If he can't walk, we'll be stuck here."

"I can." He tried again and was able to get up, but not put any weight on his left leg.

"Take his other side," I said. "We need to get him to the creek to soak his knee in the cold water." We wedged ourselves under his armpits and he hopped back towards the cave. Even with the soaking, his knee swelled more and it turned a purplish-red colour. He acted as if it didn't hurt, but he could barely put weight on it.

"He's not going to be able to walk," Sophie said.

"That helicopter is searching for us. They'll circle around. They'll definitely be back," I said.

Sophie frowned. "What if we don't want them to come back?"

"I don't think it's the drug-cartel guys. I'm sure they have way more important things to do than chase us through the wilderness for days and days."

Her shoulders relaxed a little. "Yeah, I guess Mason would have to be worth a lot of dough for them to waste those kinds of resources." She turned to face him. "Hey, Mason. Exactly how many days of searching are you worth to a Mexican drug cartel?"

He licked his lower lip and stared down at the dirt. "I'm sure they gave up after that first night."

Sophie smiled, but I knew he was lying.

I sighed and walked over to him. "Here, take these." I handed him the bag with the last four painkillers in it."

He shook his head to decline. "You need those."

"No. I don't feel pain anymore."

"Because you've been taking them."

"Mason, we might need you to be able to walk. Please take them. I'm not going to take anymore, whether you do or not, so you might as well."

He sighed to surrender and held his hand out. "I'll take two. You take the other two."

"Two won't make any difference." I tossed the bag into his palm, then turned to walk away.

"Four isn't going to make any difference either," he mumbled under his breath.

I wandered over to a tree and sat with my back against the trunk. I wanted to try to have a vision that might give me some direction or maybe warn me of danger. Nothing came to me. The only image that even flashed through my mind was from the first date I ever went on with Mason. We went to a party and it was a complete disaster. The image that was stuck in my head was a snapshot of the moment when Trevor and Mason were both staring at me, waiting for me to choose which one of them I wanted to drive me home that night.

We waited all day by the cave, taking turns, watching for a rescue team to hike in. Nobody came. We heard the helicopter two more times, but it was impossible to know if they saw the t-shirts. "We should make a signal fire while we still have daylight," I said. "They won't see the fabric at night. If it's a rescue team they'll be looking for smoke."

"If it's the cartel guys, they'll be looking for smoke too," Sophie said.

Mason's eyebrows angled together. "What if it's not a rescue team, Deri?"

"We don't really have a lot of options. Either we signal aircraft hoping for the chance that they are friendly and will help us, or Sophie and I leave you here and try to get help on our own. Which do you prefer?"

Without answering, Mason stood up and hopped around to collect dry branches. Sophie helped him by taking armfuls from him and transferring them to the shore. I separated the wood into three piles for three fires because I knew it was the international distress signal. Trevor taught me it when I was only ten. He received a survival book for his twelfth birthday and made me memorize every page with him. I gathered some dry moss and found two rocks to make a spark with. Unfortunately, I didn't have the strength to hit the rocks with the right velocity.

"Mason. I need your help."

He took the rocks out of my hands and clapped them together repeatedly. Eventually, he generated a few sparks, but not big enough to set the moss on fire. He took a break, then tried again. "Yes," he shouted.

I lunged forward and gently blew on the spark that had jumped from the rock into the moss. It started to smoke. Then when I blew again, it ignited into a small fire. "Good job." I placed it onto a bigger pile of moss, blew on it again and then transferred it to light up the first pile of sticks.

"Hey, you did it," Sophie said as she walked over to us. "Look what I found." Mason and I both glanced over our shoulders. She was holding up a bushel of purplish coloured plants. "I think we can eat these. I saw Hector's sisters taking some back to their hut."

"Yeah," Mason said and checked it out. "It's amaranth. The locals turn the seeds into a porridge-like paste." He looked around. "We could also eat acacia seeds if I can find some."

I lit the other two fires with a burning branch from the first one, then I layered damp leaves on top to make it smokier. Sophie got to work rubbing the amaranth to separate the black seeds from the plant.

"Do you want to come with me to try to find an acacia tree?" Mason asked me once the fires were smoking.

"Sure. Do you want to come, Soph?"

"I'm good. I'll keep the fire smoking and try to get enough of these to make something to eat. Just don't wander too far."

"How are you doing?" I asked him as we walked along the bank of the river.

"Good. It doesn't really hurt. It just won't bend properly."

"No, I mean, how are you really doing?"

He looked sideways at me and sort of smiled as he shook his head. "You haven't changed. You always did want to know how I really felt about things."

"And?"

He inhaled heavily and stared off into the distance. "When you weren't doing very well it reminded me of when my brother was dying. I used to have nightmares when he was sick and I've been having them again since we've been here."

"What happens in the nightmare?"

"I'm sitting on the floor in my childhood bedroom all alone. It's dark and there's no furniture in the room because my family moved out and left without me. Not only is the house empty and abandoned, the neighbourhood is also deserted." He paused and the crease between his eyebrows deepened. "When I realize that I'm all alone in the house, in the city, maybe in the world, I start to feel panicky and I can't breathe because I don't know what to do next. Then I wake up."

I stared at his face for a long time, understanding exactly how he felt. "No matter what happens, I won't leave you alone. I promise."

He hugged me tightly into his chest and rested his chin on

top of my head. After a while, I turned and pulled his arm so he would sit down with me on the grass.

"When I was delirious, I thought I saw your brother with my dad."

"I know. I heard you talking to him."

"Was he like you?"

Mason chuckled. "Everyone else thought we were exactly the same, but we didn't think we were anything alike. On our tenth birthday, our parents threw a huge party at the country club. My dad knew a guy who worked with the Toronto Maple Leafs and he gave us authentic game jerseys. We were both really excited and we put them on as soon as we opened the boxes. We wanted to know what we looked like in them, so we asked a waitress where the nearest mirror was. She laughed and told us to just look at each other if we wanted to know what we looked like in the mirror. I turned to face Cody. I thought she was a complete idiot because all I could see was how he looked in the jersey. He was the only person who saw me as Mason."

"I see you as Mason."

He smiled. "I know. That's why I can't stand the thought of losing you too. Seeing you sitting in that bar in Acapulco seriously took my breath away. All of my old feelings came flooding back as if they had never been gone." He tucked my hair behind my ear and looked into my eyes. "When I saw that you were wearing the necklace I gave you, I wondered if maybe my dreams were coming true and I was getting my second chance with you. Then you told me you and Trevor were still together. It felt like a steel blade went through my chest and stopped my heart dead."

I closed my eyes, trying to stave off the guilt. "I'm sorry."

"I'm the one who's sorry." He choked up and had to pause before he continued. "I have never felt worse than how I felt when I saw that you had been shot. I wouldn't be able to live with the guilt if anything happened to you. I'm sorry that I didn't protect you. I know Trevor would have kept you safe."

"I wouldn't be alive right now if you hadn't carried me all night."

"You wouldn't have been shot if I hadn't brought you here in the first place."

"I came here of my own free will. I'm the one who blew you're cover. Stop trying to take all the blame."

"Derian, you and Sophie would have never been in danger if it wasn't for me."

"Stop. Blaming ourselves isn't helping. We're going to make it out of this just fine. We're going to be able to look back at this and tell stories about the time we were hunted by a Mexican drug cartel. Trust me. No one will believe us, but we'll be able to tell the story."

He nodded and took a deep breath. "I just don't want to lose you," he whispered.

"You won't."

He hesitated for a long time then said, "Whether we make it out of here or not, I'm going to lose you."

I knew he was talking about me going back to Trevor if we survived. I hated how I felt in that moment. The thought of him being hurt again on top of everything else broke my heart. I wanted to say something that would make the pain on his face disappear, but I didn't know where to even start.

Eventually, he stood and held his hand out for me to join him. "Come on. Let's go find some food before it gets dark."

We didn't talk as we searched for an acacia tree. We couldn't find one nearby and we didn't want to wander too far away from Sophie, so we headed back. She was crouched next to the fire using a stick to stir a tiny bit of paste on a concave rock that she was using like a bowl. When she saw us, she hopped up and smiled. "Feel like some dinner?"

We both wandered over and dipped our finger into the paste. It actually tasted not bad, but there wasn't enough to actually satisfy any hunger. "It's really good," Mason said as he sat down near the stream.

"I can make more tomorrow," she said as she swiped her finger over the rock and licked up the last of it.

Something moved in the bushes across the stream. I tensed and turned to see if Mason heard it too. His jaw muscle twitched as he stared across the water in the direction that I'd heard the noise come from. He sprung to his feet and tugged Sophie's arm. "Get to the cave." The bush crashed as if something very large or something in large numbers, was coming towards us. We reached the base of the boulders and scrambled towards the opening of the cave. Men's voices shouted at us to stop. We were spotted.

Chapter 19

Sophie, Mason, and I all slowly turned to face the men who had just emerged out of the forest. They stood, staring at us from the opposite rocky shore of the stream. The first four men were dressed in all black with bulletproof vests and they were carrying rifle-type guns. Beside them were two other men wearing fatigues and bulletproof vests. Mason stepped to stand in front of Sophie and me like a shield. The men moved towards us and I waited for them to lift their guns and take aim. The one guy who was in fatigues was bald and so huge his vest looked like a postage stamp on his chest. The men moved quickly towards us. I let go of Mason's arm and stepped around him. My throat closed up and I had to force air in past the big lump that formed. My eyes filled with tears and I couldn't even see through the watery mess as I slid down on my butt off the rock.

I tried to run, but I fell to my knees and the heels of my hands scraped across the dirt. A bolt of pain shot through the fractured bone. I didn't care. I scrambled back to my feet and basically launched myself down the bank of the stream. I scrambled towards the men without even thinking. Although my vision was blurry from my tears, I could see the dark-haired one wearing fatigues sprint full speed at me. I hadn't even taken two steps into the water before his left arm clamped around my body. It caused excruciating pain where the bullet was lodged in me, but I bit my lip to prevent a scream from escaping. It didn't work. I screamed. The fingers of his right hand dug into my cheek and held my face so he could look directly into my eyes. I was trembling and my breath stuttered. I blinked away the tears and stared into his silvery-grey eyes. "Please tell me I'm not dreaming," I stammered between sobs.

"You're not dreaming," Trevor breathed into my ear. "I told you I would always find you, no matter where you were."

I hugged him with every ounce of strength I had left. It felt as if everything that was familiar and safe was with me. All the worry and stress that had been stored tightly in my muscles floated off my skin like a million tiny little bubbles. He leaned back to cradle my face with both his hands. We stared at each other for a long time before he smiled, which made me smile and cry at the same time. I hugged him again and rested my ear on his chest so I could hear his heart beat. "You promised you wouldn't go on any rescues until I got home. You're in big trouble, mister."

"Are sure you want to bring up the topic of trouble? If I wasn't so relieved to see you, I'd be yelling at you."

"I know. Sorry." I tilted my head back and kissed his lips softly.

He raised his eyebrow and ran his finger under my necklace pendant. "Nice necklace."

"You would notice that and not the fact that I was shot."

"What?"

I turned a little so he could see my shoulder.

"Jesus. Murph! She was shot."

I looked over towards the cave, where Murphy was already set up on the flat rock with his first-aid gear, checking Mason's bullet wound. Mason acted as if he was trying not to look at Trevor and me, but he glanced over briefly.

"Bring her over here. I'll take a look at it," Murphy hollered.

"Mason was shot too," I told Trevor.

Trevor clenched his jaw and shook his head in an angry way.

"It wasn't his fault."

"Yeah, it was."

I dug my fingers into his bicep to make him face me. "Trevor, please, we've all been through a lot. Promise you won't blame him."

"I can't promise that."

"Please."

"I can't. He nearly got you killed."

"I'm fine and he already blames himself more than he should. Promise."

Trevor looked at me suspiciously, then reached down to lift my hand up. He turned it to check if I was wearing my ring. He saw it and let my hand drop again. "I can't," he said and turned his head until he wasn't looking at my face.

"You can, and you will," I warned him.

"I'll try. I'm not making any promises."

"Seriously? We've been lost in the Mexican wilderness, shot by kidnappers, starving for days, and you want to pick a fight?"

He inhaled heavily and cracked his neck to the side, as if he was trying to get rid of his urge to go after Mason. He closed his eyes for a second, then looked directly into mine. "I'll try."

I knew I wasn't going to get a better promise than that and I was too weak to argue, so I let it go. We walked over to where everyone else was hanging out near the cave. The four guys in all black, who were obviously private security, had rested their guns on a log and were talking. Murphy examined Mason's arm. Murphy had obviously given Sophie his Search and Rescue t-shirt because she looked like she was wearing a full-length nightgown as she sat and unwrapped a protein bar.

Murphy focused on Mason, whose arm had started bleeding again. "It's not that deep. It shouldn't be bleeding like this. Do you have any medical conditions?" Murphy asked him.

Mason glanced at me before mumbling, "Not that I know of."

"Are you taking any medications?"

"No. Just two painkillers today."

I walked over and spoke softly into Murphy's ear as I hugged him, "Mason wasn't feeling well, even before this happened. He had lab work done."

"What were the results?"

"They weren't back yet," Mason murmured and shook his head at me.

Murphy finished dressing the wound with layers of gauze, then made him take some anti-inflammatory pills for his knee. He also burst two ice packs and held them in place on Mason's leg with a tensor bandage. When he was finished, he turned to me. "All right, Deri. Take a seat. Let's have a look at the damage."

I sat next to Mason on the flat rock. He didn't even look at me before he got up and hopped over to sit on the log with the guys in all black. They gave him a protein bar and Gatorade.

Murphy made a face when he looked at my shoulder. "You're lucky the bleeding stopped. This could have been really bad."

Trevor glared at me and his jaw tensed before he glanced over at Mason.

"Trevor," I warned. "I'm fine. Oh, except my wrist is broken too," I informed Murphy. "But that was from horseback riding, not from being chased by murdering drug dealers."

Murphy shook his head in a way that made it clear he didn't think my humour was appropriate.

He was right. It really wasn't appropriate given the seriousness of the situation. "I have a brace somewhere."

"Why aren't you wearing it? You've probably made it worse by now."

"It feels gross when it's wet."

"You're such a wuss."

"I took a bullet," I reminded him.

"Yeah, I guess I can give you a little credit." He shoulder-checked to see if Trevor was far enough away to not hear us. He was talking to Sophie. Murphy looked at me with dead seriousness and said in a low voice, "He's not going to let it go."

"It wasn't Mason's fault."

"Yeah, it was."

"It was my fault. I have a big mouth and I'm the reason they even found out who Mason is. I put us all in danger. He didn't do anything wrong." I stood. "I'm the one who almost got us all killed. I'm the one who Trevor should be mad at. I'm the idiot!" I didn't realize until I saw everyone staring at me that I'd been yelling. "Ugh," I growled. I was so frustrated and whatever Murphy put on my wound was making it sting. I covered my face with my hands for a few seconds.

When I looked up, they were all still studying me as if they thought I was losing it, which apparently I was. I turned, took a couple of strides, slid on my bum off the rock, and walked into the forest to calm down. I pressed my back against a tree trunk only a few metres away and sat cross-legged in the dirt. I sat there until I heard Murphy yell in his booming voice, "Hey, hey, easy."

I stood up too fast and got dizzy, so propped my hands on my knees and let my head hang down until the light-headedness passed, then I rushed back to the group. Everyone was standing near the cave. Trevor was in front of Mason and I could tell by Mason's defensive posture that Trevor had either said or done something threatening.

"I wouldn't have brought them here if I thought it wasn't safe," Mason said.

"You knew it wasn't safe," Trevor shouted. "You had a bodyguard for a reason. You used an alias for a reason. You didn't care about their safety. You just cared about trying to get laid."

"It wasn't like that."

"No? What was it like?"

"We have thirty-five volunteers and I've been down her for

four months without one single problem. I wouldn't have brought them here if I didn't believe it was completely safe."

"Yeah, that doesn't answer the question. Why did you ask her to go to the camp?"

Mason didn't answer, but whatever the look on his face was, it must have triggered Trevor because Murphy stepped in to hold Trevor back.

I climbed back up onto the rock and shouted, "Stop it. Please."

I stormed straight at Trevor. My fingernails dug into his arm as I pulled him and made him walk behind the cave with me.

Once we were alone, I said, "I specifically asked you not to get into it with him. He's injured and sick and it wasn't his fault that the kidnappers came after us."

"He was trying to move in on you. It's not cool to move in on another guy's girl."

"Excuse me. I'm not your property. I thought you trusted me."

"I do trust you. He's the problem."

"You're acting immature and I find it really unattractive. We have way bigger things to worry about than what Mason's intentions were when he invited us to the camp, which were innocent, by the way."

"Really? Are you honestly going to try and tell me that he had no intentions of winning you back?"

I didn't answer.

"See. He deserves a shit-kicking. He knows it, and you know it."

"Grow up. He's been a perfect gentleman the entire time and I didn't make it easy for him."

"What's that supposed to mean? Did something happen between you two?"

I stared at him for a while, then made a face and bit my lower lip for a second. "Sort of."

"Sort of? What the hell does that mean?"

"I sort of kissed him."

Trevor turned and walked away.

"Trev." I caught up and slid in front of him. "Don't walk away."

His eyebrows angled together. "Did you come to Mexico to see him?"

"No. I didn't know he was here. It was a coincidence."

"Really? Do you think I'm stupid? You randomly changed your trip from Tofino to Acapulco. Then you just happened to run into him while you just happened to be wearing the jewellery he gave you. It doesn't sound like a coincidence."

"I haven't even talked to Mason since you and I started dating. Sophie's dad gave us the tickets to Acapulco. It was a total coincidence. Ask them."

He inhaled heavily and then paced as he spoke, "When I heard that you and Sophie were with Mason and you were being chased by drug dealers with guns, my world felt like it was crashing down around me. The thought of you being harmed, or worse, was the most devastating thing I have ever experienced and I literally couldn't get here fast enough to find you." He paused, took a breath, and scratched the back of his neck. "When we found you and I saw you standing on that rock, it was—I can't even put it into words—it was seriously the best feeling in the universe. I never stopped thinking about you for even one second. So, to hear that you were not only, not thinking about me, but you were thinking about someone else and kissing someone else, really hurts."

"I was thinking about you," I protested. "I dreamed about you and our future together. I prayed for you to find us. I had visions about you constantly. When we had to jump off the top of a fifty-foot waterfall in the dark and I didn't know what we were going to land on, my dying wish was to kiss you one last time." I reached forward and pulled at the strap of his bulletproof vest so he would stand closer to me. "When I was delirious, Sophie and Mason told me that you wanted me to drink water and get stronger, so I did, because I thought you wanted me to. They knew you were the only person I would do it for."

"You kissed him."

"It's not exactly as bad as it sounds. I lost a lot of blood and I got a little confused. I thought you had already come to rescue us and I kissed you because I was so glad that you were here with me. Later, when I started to feel better, Sophie told me I had been hallucinating and you weren't really here. I realized that I must have kissed Mason by mistake. I thought he was you."

His expression softened. "You thought he was me?"

"Yes."

The corner of his mouth lifted in a borderline cocky smile as he stepped closer to wrap his arms around my waist. "Couldn't you tell the difference?"

"I was delirious. Give me a break." I wrapped my arms around his neck and said, "There is nothing else that I want in this world more than to be with you. You're all I have ever wanted and you're all I will ever want, but I'm not going to lie to you. I care about Mason as a friend and it's not his fault that I do. It doesn't change how I feel about you, though—you're my everything." I touched his chest above his heart.

He dropped his head down so our cheeks rested against each other. "I love you," he whispered.

A twig snapped in the forest a few metres away from us and I peeked over Trevor's shoulder as a figure slid behind a tree. I grabbed Trevor's arm and spun around so we could run back towards the security guards. They were already standing in wide stances on the rock above us and aiming their weapons at the spot in the forest where I had seen the figure go behind the tree. I heard movement behind us again and they opened fire above our heads.

Chapter 20

Trevor and I both ducked and scrambled up the rock towards the others. The figure sprinted between trees. It was a small person and I saw a flash of blue and white. The sun had already dropped behind the mountain and it was too dark in the forest to know for sure, but I thought I knew what it was. I yelled, "Stop! Stop! Stop!"

The guards didn't hear me, or didn't care that I was telling them to stop shooting. I rushed towards the guy nearest to me and pushed his rifle towards the sky. He flexed and pushed the gun across my chest, which made me fall to the ground. Then he aimed the barrel at my head. I squeezed my eyes shut and waited for him to shoot me.

"What is your dysfunction?" he shouted at me.

I opened my eyes and tried to spit out, "Stop shooting." I cringed because I thought he was going to pull the trigger. "It's a child," I muttered.

"Hold your fire," he yelled.

The shooting stopped and Mason shouted, "Stop pointing the gun at her." The guy moved the barrel so it was facing the ground next to me, but he didn't relax his hold on the trigger. "What the hell is going on?" Mason asked, furious.

"She says the target is a child."

"Derian, are you sure?" Mason asked.

"I think so. I saw what looked like a school uniform. Maybe I was wrong. I don't know. They shouldn't be shooting at something if they don't know what it is."

Mason called in Spanish out into the forest. I couldn't understand him. It sounded as if he repeated the same thing again and then there was movement behind a tree. A little boy poked his head around the trunk. He looked terrified. His mouth was wide open in a silent scream and tears ran down his cheeks. Mason said something else in Spanish.

"*Señor* Murray," the boy choked out between sobs.

"Oh, my God," I gasped and started running as I realized who it was.

Mason got to Hector before I did and scooped him up into his arms. He spoke to him in Spanish and checked his limbs to make sure he was all right.

I reached them and fell to my knees. "Hector! What are you doing here?"

Hector sniffled and used his own shirt to wipe away his tears. "Miss Darianna, I am here to help *Señor* Murray. I am the best at helping."

"Oh, my God." I wrapped my arms around both of them as Mason cradled him in his arms. "They could have killed him."

"He's okay."

"How did you get here?" I asked.

He pointed at the men in black. "I followed them. To help *Señor* Murray."

I squeezed Hector's face and said, "You're crazy brave."

"What is crazy brave?"

"It means that you are the best." I kissed his forehead, then we walked back to the cave.

Sophie rushed over to give Hector a big hug. The security guys relaxed and moved a short distance away to watch the forest.

I sat Hector down on a rock and gave him some water to drink. He took a sip, then said, "The men with guns maybe are watching. I will show the way back to the village closest to my village."

"How long does it take to get there?" Sophie asked.

"If we go when sun rises and walk the way that is not hard, after siesta. If we walk the way that is hard, before siesta."

"We would like to walk the way that is not hard," Sophie said and handed Hector a small fish-shaped origami animal that she had woven out of long blades of grass.

Hector seemed to recover fairly quickly from being shot at. Maybe because he was a kid and really didn't understand how serious it was, or maybe because Murphy was sneaking him pieces of liquorice. My heart rate still hadn't recovered. I sat on a log and Trevor gave me a protein bar and some Gatorade. When I finished that, I wolfed down two hard-boiled eggs, an apple, and an orange.

"Whoa. Slow down," Trevor said. "Your stomach isn't used to eating."

I gulped Gatorade and looked over at Mason. He was avoiding making eye contact. "Hector, do you know what happen to Orrett and the other security guards?" I asked.

He answered in Spanish and spoke quickly. He made hand gestures that looked like explosions and then he pointed to the sky in a squiggly motion. Mason mostly nodded and then asked more questions.

"Well? Is Orrett okay, or not?" Sophie asked impatiently.

"It sounds like all four of them were injured. He doesn't know if they're all right or not."

"Who's Orrett?" Trevor asked.

"He's the dentist from the camp and he's Mason's good friend. He was standing with us when the cartel guys showed up and opened fire. He got shot and we had to take off without him. There were three security guards at the camp who all took bullets for us too."

Trevor stretched his arm over my shoulder. "I'm sorry you guys had to go through that. It sounds really traumatizing."

Mason's posture tensed as if he expected Trevor to come at him again. Trevor didn't look at Mason, but the muscles in his arm twitched.

"What did Hector say about the cartel guys?" I asked.

"He doesn't know anything." Mason looked at Trevor. "What do you guys know?"

"All we were told was that the village you guys were at still wasn't secure. Your dad flew us down in a private jet with the security crew and had a helicopter fly us into a village that's about five kilometres from where you were working. The pilot had seen the fabric in the tree and we mapped out the route on foot."

"How long do you think it will take to get to that other village?" I asked, since I still wasn't very strong.

"I'm not sure. We'll have to trust the kid. We got a little lost and turned around. We probably wouldn't have found you if you hadn't lit the fires. I don't even know which way the village is from here."

"You? You got lost? I don't believe it," I poked fun at him.

"Don't sound so surprised. I was searching for a needle in a haystack in a foreign country."

"I knew you were going to get lost. I saw it in a vision. I told these guys you weren't coming for us at all. I'm actually surprised that you showed up."

He chuckled.

"How did you guys know what happened to us?" Sophie asked Murphy and Trevor.

Murphy laughed before he answered, "Some guy sent Trevor an email. It was hilarious. How'd it go?"

Trevor started talking with a surfer accent, "Dude, your girlfriend wanted me to tell you that she took off to build an orphanage or something with some guy she picked up at a bar. Tough luck. Call this number if she doesn't come back or something."

"Fortunately, Sophie had someone a little more responsible send an email to Doug," Murphy added.

I looked at Sophie. "You asked someone to send an email to Doug?"

"Duh. I wasn't going to take off into the Mexican wilderness and not let someone know where I was going. I asked Luis to send it when the internet was working again."

Trevor continued, "Luis' message to Doug mentioned what day you were supposed to be back. When I didn't hear from you, I called the hotel. When I couldn't get a hold of you, I called the number that you sent. Mason's dad had just gotten a call telling him what had happened at the camp. All he knew was that Mason had disappeared with two females. He was pretty sure you guys were still on the run in the forest, so I volunteered Murphy and me to come down. Sophie's dad flew the private jet."

"My dad's here?"

"Yeah." Trevor nodded. "He's back at the resort."

"Was he pissed?"

"Worried," Murphy said. "All of your parents are worried."

"Oh, my God," I said. "My mom's here?"

"Yup." He looked at Mason. "And your dad's at the village."

Mason's eyebrows angled together for a brief second but he didn't say anything. Murphy noticed that Mason's arm had bled through the gauze again, so he got up and redressed it. He made him drink a ton of Gatorade too. While he was drinking, his nose started to bleed. Murphy exchanged a look with Trevor and Trevor seemed to purposely avoid looking at me. I hated when they did their own private silent language.

"What?" I said softly into Trevor's ear.

"What what?"

"Why are you and Murphy exchanging knowing looks with each other?"

"Just to mess with you."

"Nice try. I'm not buying it."

"Well, I wasn't going to say anything, but we only have seven dehydrated meal packs left. Three of the security guards are going to be shit out of luck."

"Really? That's what Murphy was saying with that look?"

He nudged his shoulder against mine, trying to be light-hearted. "Yeah, wasn't it obvious?"

"Liar."

"What? It's a serious problem. They're going to have to fight over it."

"There's something's wrong with Mason, isn't there?" I whispered.

He glanced sideways at me and his face got serious. "He's going to be fine." He stood and walked over to one of their bags. "Do you want Beef Stroganoff or Mac and Cheese?" He held up two foil vacuum-packed pouches. "Just add water."

I was too distracted to answer. I watched Murphy work on Mason and bit at my fingernails. Sophie claimed a Mac and Cheese, then she sent Hector over with the one pack that the four security guards were going to have to share. Murphy tried to stifle his laughter as the sound of the guards groaning and complaining reached us.

After we ate, they turned the lanterns off and, since it was cloudy and the fires had burned themselves out, it was really dark. Hector had already curled up with his head on Sophie's lap and he was sleeping peacefully. Trevor and Mason were sitting on either side of me with their backs propped against the rock face. I slid down to rest my head on Trevor's lap. It was quiet except for the sound of the stream and the creatures in the forest.

"I know you only came for her, but I appreciate what you're doing for me too. So thanks," Mason said.

"We didn't only come for her," Trevor answered.

"Well, yeah. Sophie too."

Trevor ran his hand over my hair. "We would have come for you even if the girls weren't with you."

"Yeah right," Mason scoffed.

"We would have come for you," Trevor repeated.

"Why?"

"Because she would have asked me to."

They were all quiet after that and I fell asleep. I had Mason's nightmare. I was sitting in an empty room that had no furniture. I walked around the abandoned house and looked out the window at the vacant neighbourhood. It was cold and when I slid my palms down the glass, it left a trail of bright-red blood. Someone whispered in my ear, "I will always love you," but when I turned to see who said it, there was nobody there. I panicked.

When I woke up in the morning, Mason and one of the security guards were gone.

Chapter 21

The three remaining security guards stood close to the cave and waited for everyone to wash up and eat so we could get going. I walked up to the sandy red-headed one in charge. He crossed his arms across his chest and turned so he wasn't facing me.

"Why did Mr. Cartwright leave early?"

"Not sure," he said, without looking at me.

"Was it because he's sick?"

"Not sure," he repeated and turned to look at me with a completely cold expression.

"Is he going to meet us at the village?"

"Not sure."

"What time did they leave?"

"Not sure." He smiled at the other security guards.

"I'm glad you find this amusing. You do realize that if anything happens to him you will not only be out of a job—you'll be out of a career."

"It was his decision to leave."

"Why didn't you go with him?"

"John went with him. He gave us orders to make sure you made it back safely. I'm just following orders," he said and saluted me.

I turned and walked away from him without saying anything else. His attitude aggravated me and I didn't really have the energy to squabble with him. I shared an orange with Hector instead.

When we were ready to head out, Murphy and Trevor made Sophie and me put on their bulletproof vests.

"I would actually be more comfortable if you were wearing this since I can guarantee you will jump in front of any bullet that's coming at me," I said to Trevor.

"Don't bother arguing," he said as he tightened the Velcro.

The guards walked behind us. I felt sick almost immediately after we started hiking on an incline. It was hard to tell if it was because I couldn't handle the physical exertion, if I was anxious about running into cartel guys, or if I was upset about Mason leaving. Maybe all three. Hector walked in the lead because he knew the way, but I was uncomfortable with him being the first line of defence, so I yelled ahead, "Hector, please walk behind Murphy and tell him which way to go."

"It is better to showing the way," he protested.

"I know, but it will help you practice your English if you give directions."

"The people won't know that I am the best at saving if I am not in the first."

"You can be at the front when we get close to the village. How's that?"

His shoulders collapsed and he threw his head back in an exaggerated gesture of disappointment before he stepped aside to let Murphy pass him. He shot me a look of exasperation before falling back into line behind Murphy.

"*Gracias* Hector," I called.

The forest looked different in the day. It was actually very beautiful and I was glad to have a new memory to replace the traumatic images from the night we were chased. We paused every so often to drink and let me rest. After several hours of hiking, we stopped to have lunch.

"Do you think that John guy will be able to figure out the way to the village?" I asked Trevor.

He shrugged. "He was a Marine. I'm sure he knows what he's doing."

"It's my fault he left. I shouldn't have been affectionate with you in front of him."

"I'm your boyfriend, Deri. He needs to get over it."

"Well, wandering off in the middle of the night was a stupid way to try to get over it."

Trevor smiled and bit into an apple. "You said it, not me."

Murphy sat beside me and checked the dressing on my bullet wound. "Mason won't be able to walk that fast with his mangled knee. We'll probably catch up to them this afternoon."

"You think?"

"Yup."

I smiled and felt energized at the thought of being able to catch up to them. "Okay, let's get going." I stood and clapped my hands.

"I'm not finished eating," Trevor said.

"Eat while you walk." I pulled his hand to make him stand up.

Sophie groaned, then pushed herself off the log to follow me. "I am so going to go to the spa when we get back."

I looked over my shoulder and smiled. "Then maybe you should fly to Europe and meet up with Doug on tour."

"He probably doesn't want me to."

"I'm sure he's worried."

"I don't want to talk about it. It's going to make me cry."

I slowed down and wrapped my arm around her shoulder. "I like it when you cry."

"I don't."

We walked for hours and didn't catch up to Mason and John. It was late afternoon when we reached the base of the waterfall that Sophie, Mason, and I had jumped from. Sophie and I stopped and looked up.

"You made me jump from that!" Sophie exclaimed.

"I saw it in a vision. I knew it would be okay. Sort of."

"Sort of? Remind me not to listen to you in the future."

"We survived."

"Hey, Trevor, take our picture. I want to show Doug what we did."

Trevor pulled out his phone and turned it on to snap a photo of us standing with the waterfall in the background.

"Too bad Mason isn't here," Sophie said. "He should be in the picture too."

It made me feel really sad when she said that. My stomach cramped up and I had to hold my side. I stood buckled over for a few seconds.

"You okay?" Trevor asked.

Tears rolled down my cheeks, but I nodded.

"Do you want me to give you a piggy-back ride for a while?"

I thought about how Mason had carried me the entire distance that we had already come. I felt horrible that he had to carry me so far when he was sick and shot. "No," I answered absently. I just wanted to get going again so I could see Mason and make sure he was all right.

The sun had sunk low in the sky when Hector finally said we were close. He sprinted around Murphy to take the lead. When we reached the edge of the forest and entered a clearing where villagers could see him, Hector stood up tall and puffed his chest out. "*Hola*!" he shouted and threw his arms in the air so everyone would notice him leading us back to safety.

A bunch of people rushed towards us and patted Hector on the back. Murphy lifted Hector up on his shoulders to give him a hero's ride. I walked over to a guy who was obviously a guard and asked, "Is Mr. Cartwright here?"

He pointed to a group of men standing near a building in the middle of the clearing. It wasn't Mason. It was his dad. He looked up from the device he had in his hand. He smiled and excused himself from the group before walking over to me. "Derian. Thank God." He hugged me. "I'm very sorry you got mixed up in this. How are you doing?"

"Okay, I guess. Where's Mason?"

"What do you mean? Isn't he with you?" He looked behind me, searching for Mason.

"No. He left before us with one of the guards. He should be here already." I left Mr. Cartwright and ran back to Trevor. "Mason hasn't made it back yet."

Trevor and Murphy exchanged one of their looks.

"It's going to get dark soon." The tone of my voice rose with my panic. "What if they got lost?"

"Maybe they went to the other village," Trevor said calmly.

Mr. Cartwright had followed me and stood next to Murphy. "Is it safe at the other village?" I asked him.

"No." He shook his head. "We were able to get security in to evacuate the volunteers, but the cartel men are still in the area somewhere. I've pulled everyone out of the project. Only locals and a few people from the medical team are still there."

"Can we contact them to see if Mason is there?"

"I'll try." He walked away and talked with a guard.

Trevor wrapped his arms around me and whispered, "He's fine."

"You don't know that." I started to hyperventilate.

A few minutes later, Mason's dad came back and shook his head. "We can't make contact right now in case the lines are being monitored."

"Would it be possible for us to take a helicopter there? We can check if Mason's there and return Hector to his family," I proposed.

"Hector?"

"He's one of the kid's Mason has been helping. He found us in the forest and led us here." I directed Mr. Cartwright to where Hector was telling stories to some local boys. "Hector, I would like you to meet *Señor* Murray's father."

"*Hola Señor* Murray. I am crazy brave."

"So I've heard. *Gracias*. How would you like to go for a ride in a helicopter?"

"Like whoo whoo whoo?" he asked and spun his finger around in a circle to imitate the blades.

Mr. Cartwright nodded with an enthusiastic smile.

"No!" Hector shook his head from side to side.

"It's fun," I encouraged. "We will all go with you and your family will see that you are the hero."

He looked at me in suspicious contemplation, then the helicopter actually showed up. It dropped down into the clearing and sent sand and leaves whirling at us.

"What do you think? Are you brave enough?" Mr. Cartwright asked.

"Okey dokey," Hector agreed.

Trevor, Murphy, Sophie, and I climbed into the helicopter behind Mr. Cartwright and Hector. It only took a few minutes to pop over to Hector's village. We climbed out, and a woman I assumed was his mom came running with her arms open wide. It made me tear up to see them reunited.

Mr. Cartwright instructed the pilot to keep the engine running while he checked for Mason. Sophie and I ran to our tent to get our bags. On the way back to the helicopter, the nurse rushed towards me with a paper in her hand. "Derian!"

I stopped and gave my bag to Sophie and told her I'd meet her at the helicopter.

"Could you please give this to Bill and tell him that he needs to see a doctor immediately," the nurse said.

"He hasn't been here?"

"No. Isn't he in the helicopter?"

"We got separated. I was hoping he was here."

She shook her head and looked very concerned. "He needs to see a doctor as soon as possible."

"Is it really bad?"

She smiled with tight lips and hugged me. "They're waiting for you."

I looked over my shoulder. Mr. Cartwright was half-hanging out of the helicopter and waving for me to hurry.

"Take care," I said to the nurse and ran to Mason's tent. I grabbed the wind chime off the post outside, then crawled inside the tent through the flap. There was a backpack hanging from a hook. I stuffed the wind chime in it and searched for the letters that he'd written to me. I found the stack of envelopes stuffed between his foam bedroll and the wooden bed frame. I also saw a drawing tacked on the tent post. I pulled it down and looked at it more closely. It was a sketch of me. I stuffed that and a few items that I thought looked important into the bag before I rushed back out. I ran to the helicopter and the pilot literally lifted off the ground the second that both my feet were inside. I sat down and unfolded the piece of paper the nurse had given me. It was Mason's blood-test results. I didn't know what any of the categories meant, but I could see that his numbers were either way higher or way lower than the normal range that was printed beside them.

I handed it to Murphy and made a confused expression. As he read it, his eyebrows angled together and the creases on his bald head deepened. He folded the paper and gave it back to me. I gestured with my palms out and shrugged so he would know I was waiting for an explanation. He glanced over at Mr. Cartwright, back at me, then out the side window. I kicked the toe of his boot, but he ignored me. Trevor, who had been watching the entire exchange, avoided making eye contact with me once he knew I was looking at him.

We flew back to the other village and the helicopter touched down in the clearing. Mr. Cartwright hopped out first and talked to the pilot. I turned to Murphy and stared him down. I didn't even have to ask him, he just spoke, "I'm not a doctor, Deri. He needs to talk to a doctor."

"But what do you think it is?"

"Could be lots of things. His medical information is confidential and it's none of our business. You shouldn't have even looked at it."

He climbed out of the helicopter and I tried to follow, but Trevor pulled my arm and pushed me back down on the seat.

"Derian, you have to go to the hospital."

"No! I'm not leaving."

"You are!" he shouted, then he took a deep breath to force himself to speak more calmly. "You and Sophie need to go back to Acapulco, where it's safe. We'll meet you there as soon as we find Mason. He's probably really close. It won't take that long."

"No. I'm not leaving without him."

"You'll only slow me down. I can find him faster if I don't have to worry about keeping you safe too. Please do it for me."

"I'll keep up. I can't leave him."

"Deri! You won't want to be there if—" He stopped himself and stared at me.

"If what? If he's dead?"

He kissed me. "I'll find him for you. He's going to be fine. I promise."

I pushed past him and jumped out of the helicopter.

"Get back in the helicopter," Trevor shouted.

Murphy caught me and threw me over his shoulder. I pounded the heel of my hand against his back and kicked my legs, but he acted as if he couldn't even feel the blows.

"Let go of me! I promised him I wouldn't leave him alone!" I screamed.

Murphy literally chucked me into the helicopter and I landed on my ass on the floor. It actually hurt a lot and stunned me. The helicopter took off as I scrambled to get to my feet. I lunged towards the door, but we were already too high to jump. Sophie pulled me back by the waistband of my shorts and made me sit down beside her.

As the helicopter tilted and flew above the trees, something dinged off the front window of the helicopter and put a hole in the glass. The pilot banked abruptly and got us higher fast. He spoke into his headset and changed the direction we were flying in.

"What the hell was that?" Sophie asked me.

I leaned forward and looked more closely at the hole in the window. It was hard to see because the only light was coming off the controls. "I think it was a bullet."

"Shit," she mumbled quietly and turned her face so I couldn't see her expression.

The cartel men were obviously really close to the village and I became hysterical at the realization that Trevor, Mason, and Murphy were all in grave danger. I couldn't actually deal with the reality of losing all of them, so I pretended it was just a horrible dream. To distract myself, I opened Mason's backpack and pulled out the stack of envelopes that each had my name scribed in Mason's neat handwriting across the front. I opened the one at the bottom of the pile, turned on a light above my head, and started to read. My hands shook so badly it seemed as if the words danced across the page. The letter was a page and a half long and he had written it on the bus on the way to the camp when he first arrived in Mexico. It was obvious he was excited and scared at the same time. He didn't know anyone at that point.

I finished the first one and folded it back into the envelope. I suddenly realized that I might have just seen Trevor for the last time. A weird whimpering sound came out of my throat and I was practically convulsing. I opened Mason's second letter to prevent myself from jumping out of the helicopter in desperation. It was four pages long. It described everything about the camp and the locals. He mentioned that he had met an interesting kid named Hector, who had given him a woven leather belt and said with a big grin, "Welcome gringo."

As I finished the second letter, I heard the pilot telling someone on the radio where the shots had been fired from and how close it was to the village. I couldn't bear listening, so I opened the next envelope and plugged my ears with my fingers as I read. The third and fourth letters introduced me to a bunch of different volunteers. It described their backgrounds and what brought them to volunteering in Mexico. Mason was fascinated by all of the different lives that people lived. He explained their personalities in detail to me. I felt as if I had actually met them.

By the fifth letter, it seemed like he missed home a little. His tone sounded sad and he wrote about some of the things he didn't like about the camp. I was interrupted because we were hovering above the hospital and about to land. There were still about twenty more letters that I had to read, so I packed them in my bag to look at later.

Chapter 22

The helicopter landed on the roof of the hospital and we were met by a security guard, who escorted us in. A nurse took Sophie and me into an examination room and cleaned up all of our scrapes and gashes while a doctor treated my bullet wound.

"They'll be fine," Sophie reassured me and held my hand.

"Mason's sick with something and nobody will tell me what it is."

"He doesn't look sick. I'm sure he'll be fine."

"Ow!" I winced as the doctor stuck a needle into my back. A few minutes later, I could feel him dig around to get the bullet out. Obviously, the needle had a fair amount of anaesthetic in it because it didn't hurt anymore. Eventually, I heard a metal clank as the bullet dropped into a pan.

"Do you want to keep it?" he asked.

"No."

"I will," Sophie said. "Do you care?"

I shook my head, too depressed to care. The doctor stitched the wound and bandaged it back up. The entire procedure was surprisingly quick and easy. I was able to walk out of the examining room as if nothing had even happened. I felt so guilty for being perfectly fine while, for all I knew, they were all dead.

Mr. Cartwright had arranged for an SUV to take us back to the resort. It was waiting for us out front. During the ride back to the hotel, I read more letters. Mason wrote about the construction of the school and visiting the ancient ruin for the first time. He went on about how he thought I would love to see the ruin in person. He also described the resort in Acapulco.

My reading was interrupted again when Sophie said, "I want to see Doug."

I put the letter down and hugged her. "As soon as we get back to the resort, we'll check where the band is right now. Maybe your dad can arrange to get you a flight to meet up with them at their next stop."

"I was so mean to him. What if he doesn't want to see me?"

"He loves you. He'll understand why you pushed him away. I know he'll be happy to see you."

When we pulled up in front of the resort, my mom and Jim were standing in the lobby. I jumped out of the truck before it even stopped rolling and ran to them. My mom made a coughing sound as she tried to hold back her tears.

Sophie's parents and Kailyn were seated on benches a few feet away. They hadn't noticed us yet. And standing next to the lobby desk, with his back up against the wall, wearing dark jeans, shit-kicker boots, and a leather jacket, was Doug. I let go of my mom and spun around to see if Sophie had spotted him yet. It took her about two seconds before she saw him. His mouth smiled but his eyes were tearing up. She shrieked and ran across the lobby. He rushed to meet her and their bodies collided. She wrapped her legs around his waist and he swung her around. When they paused to stare at each other, they looked so in love. It made me happy and really sad at the thought that I had already had my reunion and might not get another chance at it.

I hugged Kailyn and Jim before I filled everyone in on what had happened. Jim looked tenser than I had ever seen him look. I hadn't even mentioned the fact that the helicopter was shot at as we left. If he knew that, he would have probably rushed out to rescue them himself.

"Is Trevor lost?" Kailyn asked me.

"No. He's finding Mason for me. Then they're both going to come here."

My mom's arms wrapped around me. She always knew something tragic was going to happen to Trevor one day. She knew he would risk his own life for someone else one too many times and I would lose him forever. I murmured, "I'm sorry. I messed up so bad."

I waited for her to agree, but instead she reassured me, "They'll be back soon."

Orrett hobbled into the lobby on crutches. I let go of my mom and ran to him. "Sophie!" I yelled and slowed down so I wouldn't knock him over. I gingerly gave him a hug.

"Hey, you're alive!" He beamed.

"So are you!" I exclaimed.

Sophie rushed over to us and hugged him. His wife and son came in behind him, so he introduced us and then we made him meet our families.

"Where's Bill, or Mason, I should say?"

I bit my lower lip and clenched my eyes shut.

"What? Is he okay?"

"I don't know. We were separated and he didn't make it back to the camp. They're still searching for him." I pulled out Mason's lab results and handed them to Orrett to look at. "What do these mean?"

He frowned at them for a while before handing the paper back to me.

"What?" I asked.

"He needs to see a doctor."

Chapter 23

It was frustrating that nobody would tell me what was wrong with Mason, but they didn't really need to since it was obviously something bad.

My mom led me up to her room where I showered and changed into fresh clothes. Then I called my granddad. He was extremely worried, so I pretended to sound optimistic. I could tell he didn't buy it and after I hung up I laid on the bed staring at the ceiling in a depressed stupor.

"You should try to eat something," my mom said and rested her hand on my shoulder.

"I'm not hungry."

"Well, at least come down and sit with everyone. You might be able to eat some salad or something."

I knew I couldn't eat, but I hoped being around everyone else would distract me from the worse-case-scenario reel that was playing in my head repeatedly. I stood and followed her to the elevator like a zombie. My brain was in a total fog and every time I blinked, I saw images of being in the forest. It already seemed like a dream that didn't really happen. I couldn't remember getting from the elevator to the restaurant, but I must have because when I looked around I was sitting at a table with my mom, Jim, Kailyn,

Sophie, and Doug. They all had plates piled high with food and they were deep in conversation with each other.

Jim got up from the table and came back with a milkshake that he put down in front of me. "Try this, Deri. You need to eat something."

"Thanks." I stared at the milkshake for a while, then got up and wandered outside in a daze. The path that I ended up on was the one Mason and I had taken from the nightclub to the beach. I stared at the paving stones thinking about how, only a few days earlier, his feet had stepped in that exact spot.

My thoughts drifted again into memories, both good and bad. I sat on the sand where Mason and I had hung out. I picked up a handful and let the grains run through my fingers. I wasn't sure if a vision would be that helpful since the terrain they were in wasn't familiar to me, but I wanted to try. Unfortunately, nothing happened.

"Hey."

I looked over my shoulder. Doug was standing above me, silhouetted by the moonlight. "Hey."

He threw his leather jacket on the sand, then sat down next to me and stared out at the ocean. "Do you want to talk?"

I shrugged. "What's there to say?"

"Nothing, I guess." He stared out over the water. "Just wanted to make sure you know I'm here for you too."

"Thank you." I reached over to give him a hug. "Did the band have to cancel some shows for you to be here?"

"We rescheduled them."

"Sorry."

He shook his head to dismiss my concern. "It's not your fault."

I raised my eyebrow and dug my heels into the sand.

"Trevor and Murphy are going to find him."

I sighed. "Do you ever wish we could just go back to being kids again, when life wasn't so complicated?"

"No. I like being an adult—even if it's hard sometimes."

"Rock stars aren't really adults," I teased, and shoved his shoulder, then I sighed at the thought that three people I cared about were still in danger. "Is Sophie the only girl you've ever loved?"

He nodded. "Yes, and she's the person I want to be with forever."

"Forever is a long time."

"Yeah, but I can hardly breathe when we're not together, so that's how long it's going to have to be."

I closed my eyes and nodded. "I know how you feel."

He squeezed his arm around my shoulder and we sat like that until Sophie found us. They invited me to go for a walk with them but I didn't feel like it. Instead, I headed back to the room to get Mason's letters, then I went to the lobby and hung out on the couches. I hoped that reading them might trigger a vision about where he was, but I was also a little reluctant to have a vision since they usually signalled something traumatic. Maybe no intuition news was good news.

At midnight my mom took Kailyn upstairs to sleep in her room and Jim hung out with me. It was quiet in the hotel after the nightclub closed. The waves crashing on the beach were the only sound I heard as I read more of Mason's letters. Jim rested his head back on the leather couch and drifted to sleep with his legs stretched out in front of him.

When morning arrived, the staff set up the breakfast buffet. A few guests walked through the lobby. Some looked as if they were going for a jog and some were dressed for a swim. I was so tired, but I refused to let my eyelids close for longer than a second. I vowed to not rest until I knew they were all safe. That was my punishment. I also decided that if they didn't all make it back safe I would punish myself more severely.

At about nine o'clock, a black SUV pulled up in front of the hotel. I sprung to my feet and ran to the curb. Mr. Cartwright stepped out, but no one else was with him.

"Did they find him?"

He shook his head with a grim seriousness. "I haven't heard anything yet."

My stomach hurt so badly I had to clutch my side. The pain made me buckle over. I must have scared Jim because he was next to me in moments. "What is it, Deri?"

I couldn't speak.

"We haven't heard from them yet," Mr. Cartwright answered for me. "I had to leave because we heard more shots being fired. It wasn't safe for me to be in the village. The helicopter will be close and on stand-by. We'll get them out of there as soon as they show up."

Jim bent over and lifted my arms to drape them around his neck. Then he slid his arm under my knees to pick me up. "You need to get some sleep."

"No."

He didn't argue with me, he just carried me to the elevator and took me to my mom's room. He put me down gently on the bed and covered me with the blanket.

"Come on, Kiki, let's go get some breakfast," he said and they left.

My mom didn't say anything. She just sat down on the bed beside me and rubbed my back. I fought to stay awake so I could continue punishing myself. I tried to have a vision that would help me see what was going to happen, but my body betrayed me and I fell asleep. I had a series of nightmares, none of which made any sense, except the one of Mason walking with his brother through a grassy field. At one point, I abruptly woke up and I could hear screams in my throat straining to escape from behind my tightly closed lips. My mom moved to hug me. "Shh. It's going to be okay, sweetheart."

Without speaking I rolled out of bed, stumbled down the hall, and took the elevator back down to the lobby. I sat on the leather couch and waited. I vaguely remembered Sophie sitting with me for a while. Jim was in and out. My mom tried to get me to eat, but I was basically unresponsive to all of them. I stared out at the curb and waited for a black SUV to pull up.

It got dark outside again and guests who were all dressed up walked by to go for dinner. Eventually, the bass from the nightclub started up. It got late and I'd been alone for a while when Kailyn sat down beside me and put her hand on mine. "Don't be scared. When you're scared it makes me scared," she said. Tears pooled up in her silvery-grey eyes.

I saw Trevor in her eyes and I immediately snapped out of my stupor, for her sake. "Okay. Do you want to get something to eat with me?"

"Yes. I like the midnight buffet. They have giant shrimps."

"Sounds good." I dragged myself off the couch and into the dining room. I knew Trevor would have wanted me to be strong for her. It was the least I could do.

"When will Trevor and Murphy find Mason Cartwright?" She asked as we walked along the buffet table.

"Soon."

"Is Trevor going to be mad at him for getting lost in the forest?"

"No. He's just worried, not mad." I sat down at a table with a plate full of food and stared at it.

"If Trevor doesn't come back will you be sad?"

"He's coming back, Kailyn. He will always come back."

"If Mason doesn't come back will you be sad?"

I nodded and swallowed back my emotions. "I'll be devastated."

She popped a shrimp in her mouth. "What does devastated mean?"

"It means the worst-possible sadness."

She nodded as if she understood exactly what that meant, which only broke my heart more.

When she finished eating, she headed up to my mom's room. I left my full plate on the table and went to sit in the lobby. I must have fallen asleep again because the next thing I remembered was waking up when someone touched my hand. I opened my eyes. Jim sat beside me on the couch. As soon as I saw the expression on his face, I knew something was wrong and I bolted up. My insides felt as if they were caving in. "What is it? Just tell me."

"We heard from the camp," he said seriously.

"Is he dead?"

"He's not dead. They just can't find him and they need your help. You need to try to see where he is." He gently lifted my chin with his finger. "You need to try to see where he is before it's too late. They can't do it without you."

Chapter 24

After Jim told me I was the only hope for finding Mason, I got up and walked away from him. I grabbed an apple from the buffet table to try to give myself some strength, then wandered around the resort to find a quiet place to focus and have a vision. I still worried it wouldn't help much since anything I saw would probably just look like Mexican forest and wouldn't give any clues to where Mason was. But I was determined to try.

I sat on the sand where Mason and I had hung out on that first night. I cupped my hands to hold the sand. Then I let the tiny white grains trickle between my fingers. It seemed almost as if I could smell Mason and feel the warmth of his body next to mine. I closed my eyes and listened to the waves rolling up on the beach. I heard him laughing when we were in the mess hall at the camp. I saw him frowning when I told him that I was still with Trevor. I also felt his heart beat against my chest. The images started to flash at a disorienting speed. He was sitting next to me on the bus smiling as we talked about Britannia Beach; leading me through the ancient ruins; carrying me through the forest on his back; keeping me warm in the cave.

I opened my eyes and stared out at the ocean. An hour passed, and despite extreme concentrated effort, I didn't have a vision. I needed to try something different—maybe if I touched his dad's hand. I got up and rushed to go find Mr. Cartwright.

An elderly woman approached me along the garden path. "That's a beautiful pendant," she said as she passed by me. I pressed my hand to my chest and held the pendant. It triggered a vision: Mason was in a meadow with his brother. He was lying in the grass staring up at the sky. Cody was sitting beside him keeping him company. He looked up and pointed at a stone pyramid at the edge of the clearing. He smiled and then disappeared.

My eyesight came back into focus and there was a cute guy standing in front of me. He chuckled. "You okay?"

"I have epilepsy. Excuse me." I rushed past him and ran to the lobby to find Jim. "I saw a pyramid. He's in a meadow somewhere near a pyramid."

Jim quickly unfolded a map on the coffee table. He pointed. "This is where the team is right now. This is where they found you. This is where the village is." We both scanned the area around that to see if there were any open grassy areas or ruins. We both spotted it at the same time. He stood and took the map over to where Mr. Cartwright was. Mr. Cartwright frowned and shook his head. Jim became tense and his voice got louder. I stood and walked over to them.

"I'm not sending the team on a wild-goose chase because Derian has a feeling that's where he is," Mr. Cartwright said.

"It's not a feeling. She sees things," Jim said.

"Sees things? What does that mean?"

"Listen, I can't explain it, but I've witnessed her do it before. She has strong intuition and she's saved lives doing it."

"I don't have time for this. If you have some legitimate Search and Rescue advice I'll take it into consideration, but I'm not going to take a hunch that a girl who thinks she's psychic has."

"You don't have to send your team if you don't want, but I'm sending Trevor and Murphy. Put me in contact with them."

Mr. Cartwright shook his head in disagreement but handed his phone to Jim. Jim paced around and gestured with his hands as he explained everything over the phone. He hung up and gave the phone back to Mr. Cartwright. He winked at me, then walked over and stretched his arm across my shoulder. "Good girl. They'll find him before it gets dark again."

I went through another night in exactly the same way—a wreck. Jim must have carried me up to my mom's room again because I woke up to the sound of the key card sliding through the lock. The door opened slowly. To my absolute relief Trevor stepped into the room.

I jumped up off the bed and bounded across the room to leap into his arms. He hugged me tightly and I felt the tension leave his body. "Is everybody okay?"

"Yeah." He leaned back to kiss me and then smiled, as if he thought I was amazing. "We found him right where you said he would be."

My eyes blinked slowly with the weight of the worry releasing. "Where is he now?"

"At the hospital."

"He's hurt?"

"No. They just got lost when they went too far south and walked past the village. He's at the hospital to treat the dehydration and to follow up on those test results."

"How long will he be there?"

"Until this afternoon probably."

I wrapped my arms tighter around his shoulders and leaned in to whisper in his ear, "Thanks for finding him."

"You're welcome, but you found him." He lifted me off the ground in a bear hug. "We couldn't have done it without your help."

I smiled with pride and then wrinkled my nose as he placed me back on the ground. "You need a shower."

His eyebrow shot up in a mischievous way. "Your mom gave me her key and headed off to the beach. We have the place to ourselves for a while if you'd like to join me."

I pulled my t-shirt off over my head and unbuttoned my shorts before I spun around and raced him to the bathroom.

My mom stayed at the beach all morning to give Trevor and me some privacy, which was unusually cool of her. She preferred to believe that I was still a virgin and that I would be one until I got married, so normally Trevor and I had to sneak around to be together. The fact that she was willing to accept our relationship made me realize it was probably time for me to be cool about her and Ron's relationship.

Trevor was asleep, so I sat cross-legged on the bed next to him and read the rest of Mason's letters. He wrote about how he had started feeling sick and he was telling me about how he wasn't that concerned, but obviously he sort of was, or he wouldn't have mentioned it in the letter. His last letter was written a week before he ran into us in Acapulco. I read it twice. He described the symptoms he'd been having and he mentioned how Orrett and the nurse were insisting that he get blood tests done. He was scared because they were the same symptoms Cody had had before they found out he had cancer, and because they were twins the nurse was concerned that he might have the same thing. The last line was: *Derian, if I could wish for anything, it would be for you to be here with me so I would have someone to talk to. I know we can't be together, but I don't want to be alone. I miss you, Love Mason.*

My tears dripped down onto the letter and made the ink run.

"You okay?" Trevor asked as he rolled over and placed his hand on my leg.

"He's sick," I said and turned to make eye contact with him. "I have to go to him."

Trevor nodded as if he already suspected I would want to. "I know."

"Thank you for understanding." I leaned over and kissed him, then got off the bed and grabbed Mason's backpack. "I love you."

"Love you, too."

I left the room and headed down to the lobby. Mr. Cartwright was standing near the door, talking on his phone, so I waited for him to finish.

When he hung up, I smiled and asked, "Is Mason back yet?"

"Why?" His tone seemed unnecessarily short.

"Because I want to see him."

He made a strange face and rubbed his chin. "Uh, Derian. He asked me to tell you that he doesn't want to see you."

"What?"

His phone rang, so he said, "Excuse me."

That didn't make sense. I was almost positive Mason wouldn't have said that. Or, if he did, he didn't mean it. If he did mean it, I needed to hear it directly from him. I waited until Mr. Cartwright was off the phone and approached him. "I appreciate everything you've done for us, Mr. Cartwright, and I know that you're just trying to protect him, but with all due respect you don't know him as well as I do."

He didn't seem impressed with the accusation and he didn't say anything before he turned and walked out the door.

Mason was obviously in the hotel somewhere, so I rushed over to the double doors that led to the kitchen, searching for Luis. He wasn't in the kitchen, so I wandered around on the pool deck and finally found him by the hot-tub bar. "Hey Luis. I need a favour."

"Anything."

"Could you find out which room Mason Cartwright is staying in? His dad would have booked all the rooms at the same time."

"Sure."

"And I'll need you to give me a key too."

He looked at me suspiciously. "I could get fired."

"Oh, then never mind."

He smiled. "Just kidding."

I slid the card through the lock on the door and the light flickered green. I turned the knob and pushed the door open as I knocked. It was dark in the room because the curtains were drawn. I walked through the living room towards the double doors that led to the bedroom. The doors were open wide. The bed was empty and still neatly made. The light wasn't on in the bathroom. It felt weird. Although it looked like he wasn't in the bedroom, I could feel that he was.

I closed my eyes and listened for his breathing. He was seated on the floor with his head propped up against the side of the bed, looking at the wall. He didn't even get startled, he just stretched his arm out so I would join him on the floor. I grabbed the pillows off the bed and propped them behind his head, then slid down next to him.

"I have the same cancer my brother died from."

I sighed and reached over to hold his hand. "They have better treatments now than they did then. And your dad will pay for the best treatments possible."

"He doesn't know yet."

"Do you want me to tell him?"

"No, maybe just be with me when I do." He inhaled deeply and tightened his arm around my shoulder. "How did you know?"

"I could tell that Murphy was concerned when your wounds wouldn't stop bleeding. Then the nurse gave me your lab results and she said you needed to see a doctor as soon as possible. Then I read the letters that you wrote to me."

"Really?" He sat up straighter. "You went back to the camp?"

I reached for his bag and pulled out the wind chime, the letters, and the picture he had sketched of me. "We took Hector back and I picked up some of your stuff. Thank you for the letters. I loved every one."

He exhaled heavily and rested his head against the mattress again. "I'm going to miss the people in the village."

"I know." I smiled as I remembered. "You should have seen Hector when he led us into the village. He got a hero's welcome and he soaked it up. Maybe when you get better we can go back to visit him together."

I watched his chest rise and fall a couple of times as he breathed. "I might not get better, Derian."

"You do."

"Cody didn't."

"You do." I moved to sit facing him. "I know you do because a long time ago I had a vision of my wedding day. You were there and you gave me two really amazing wedding gifts. I'm not planning to get married until I graduate, and, as you know, it takes a long time to become an architect. Obviously, you're going to be around for a long time."

He chuckled. "What do I give you? You can save me the hassle of shopping around."

"It's a surprise, but I'll give you a hint. One, is my all-time favourite car. The other one you promised to give me on our very first date."

He thought for a second then said, "A '63 Corvette Stingray and a trip to New York to visit the Guggenheim. Those are good gifts."

"Yes, they are. And too generous, so don't actually give them to me."

He nodded, but I knew he'd try. "Does Trevor know you're here?"

"Yes, and he understands."

"Of course he does." He sighed and then got up to sit on the edge of the bed, with his elbows rested on his knees. "You made the right choice with him."

"What you and I have is really special in a different way. I need you in my life, as a friend," I said and turned my head so I could see his face. "You do realize that I'm going to go with you to every one of your treatments and make you drink highly nutritious vegetable-and-wheat grass concoctions from the juicer."

"That's good because I don't have anyone else."

"Yes you do. Your parents—"

He cut me off. "My mom didn't even come down here to make sure I was all right."

"Maybe the thought of losing another son was just too difficult for her to face."

"I'm not lost. I'm here."

"Well, I'm here. And Sophie, Murphy, Doug, and Trevor would all lie down in front of a truck for you, too. Don't ever think they wouldn't."

"They would be doing it for you, not me."

"No. They would do it for you. You will never be alone. I promise."

He didn't say anything, but he seemed to feel better.

I moved to sit next to him and needled his ribs gently. "I knew I would be able to convince you to come home."

He chuckled. "You do have a way of getting what you want. It's quite a talent."

"Mmm. Almost as slick as Chance Cartwright."

"Almost."

"While we're on the topic of me getting what I want, I believe you owe me a day at the spa and a thousand dollars for the Liam email bet."

"I can arrange that." His head turned and he smiled. "And then what?"

"And then I want you to get better."

He nodded. "You got it."

I stretched my arm across his shoulder and squeezed. "Thanks."

There was a knock on the door, so I stood and crossed the room to peek through the peephole. I assumed it would be his dad. When I saw who it was, I smiled and opened the door. Sophie and Doug stepped in with arms full of snacks, followed by Murphy, Kailyn, Orrett, his wife and their son, and Trevor.

"Thank you," I whispered to Trevor and squeezed his hand as Mason appeared at the bedroom doorway with a touched expression in his eyes.

"I'm glad you aren't lost anymore, Mason Cartwright," Kailyn said as she hugged him around the waist. Then everyone else hugged him too.

It really couldn't have been a happier ending.

The End

Acknowledgements

This is the third book in the series and it's been an amazing adventure from start to finish. I am forever grateful to Charlotte Ledger and the team at Harper*Impulse* for seeing the potential in my stories and working with me to make the vision a reality. Thank you to my husband Sean for encouraging me to keep writing even when nobody was reading. Thank you to my critique partner Denise Jaden, Greg Ng (and the students and moms from his class who volunteered to read a very early rough draft of Britannia Beach), Rasadi Cortes, Erica Ediger, Jen Wilson, Belinda Wagner, Lisa Marks, Cory Cavazzi, my mom and dad, my brother Rob, my sister Luan, and the entire team behind the scenes at Harper*Impulse* and HarperCollins *Publishers*. I'd also like to send a special thank-you to the real Search and Rescue volunteers and first responders in the Squamish area, and the young adult bloggers and youth librarians who tirelessly introduce books to young readers.